DKW B4 G 75

'If you were but a year or two older I would carry you hence if I had to kill every man here to do it! I mean to have you, my lady. I shall return to claim you one day . . .'

Now it is 1486, and with the ending of the bloody Wars of the Roses the proud Lord Alvar has come to claim his bride. The Lady Elspeth Murran was barely fifteen years old when she first set eyes on the man known as the Wolf of Alvar, yet she was fascinated by him. Now her fascination is tempered by fear for the mystery that lies in his past. When she learns the truth, can she accept the terrible secret that had been hidden in his heart, or will it destroy her love?

By the same author in Masquerade

DEVIL'S KIN

MILLS & BOON LIMITED
London · Sydney · Toronto

First published in Great Britain 1983
by Mills & Boon Limited, 15–16, Brook's Mews,
London W1A 1DR

ISBN 0 263 74191 5

04/0283

Set in 10 on 10½pt Linotron Times

Photoset by Rowland Phototypesetting Ltd
Bury St Edmunds, Suffolk
Made and printed in Great Britain by
Cox and Wyman Ltd, Reading

CHAPTER ONE

FROM the seaward side Murran Castle seemed to rise out of a sheer wall of granite, its frowning presence a landmark for sailors blown off course by the fury of the north-east winds. For more than a hundred years it had guarded England against attack, both from the sea and across the border with Scotland.

Balancing precariously on the edge of her sister's dower chest, the Lady Elspeth Murran peered through the narrow, slitted window of the west tower. In the distance she could see a troop of horsemen approaching. Fluttering proudly in the breeze was a pennant of gold, boldly stamped with the head of a snarling wolf. All the men wore the black and gold livery of the house of Alvar—except one. He rode at their head, dressed in severest black, his rich velvet cloak lined with fur.

Lady Elspeth gave a crow of delight. 'I can see him. I can see the Wolf of Alvar,' she cried triumphantly, rewarded at last for her hours of patient watching. 'Oh, Nan, I vow he is every bit as fierce and wicked as Nessie said he would be!'

The Lady Nanette laid down her embroidery, shaking her head in mild disapproval as she saw the gleam of excitement in her sister's dark eyes. 'Pray come down before you fall and hurt yourself, Elspeth,' she said. 'You will have chances enough to see Lord Alvar in the next few days.'

Elspeth slid from her vantage point and ran to her elder sister's side. Kneeling beside her, she took Nanette's hand and pressed it to her cheek.

'I wish he had not come,' she declared passionately,

her lovely face marred by the sulky downturn of her full red lips. 'I wish none of them had come. I wish you were not to be married to Alvar's kinsman. Oh, Nan, what shall I do when you are gone?'

Lady Nanette stroked her sister's thick curls, sighing as she saw the signs of a storm in the girl's face. At fourteen Elspeth already showed the promise of great beauty, her eyes lustrous and glowing with an inner fire. A fire which was all too likely to spill over in a torrent of wild passion whenever she was roused to anger, burning itself out quickly and leaving Elspeth repentant and wretched.

Elspeth was as dark as their father and half-brothers, while Nanette had the pale fairness of their mother. The Lady Elizabeth had died soon after Elspeth was weaned, worn out by childbirth and endless miscarriages as she tried to give her husband the male heir he craved; beaten at last by the bleakness of her life in the castle with a man she had come to hate.

It was Nanette who cared for Elspeth as she lay forgotten and neglected in her cot, though she herself was but a child of twelve. Helped by their old nurse, Bethany, she had raised her sister in the face of the Earl's indifference.

He had shown only annoyance when his wife died so soon after the birth of yet another daughter. Taking one look at the mewling infant, he abandoned her to her fate. So many of his off-spring had died in infancy that perhaps he believed Elspeth would die too. Certainly he had no use for a second daughter, nor a wife who died without fulfilling her duty. Within three months of her death he married again; a sturdy, healthy woman called Margaret, who lost no time in providing him with twin boys.

Finding in the Lady Nanette a streak of stubbornness belied by her meek manner, the new Countess followed her husband's lead and ignored his daughters whenever possible. They were adequately clothed and fed; and when the Earl was obliged to take the widow of an impoverished kinsman into his household, Nessie saw to it that they received the sketchy education deemed necessary for their role in life. Which was, it seemed, to keep out of the Earl's way, and in Nanette's case, to be at the beck and call of her stepmother increasingly as she grew to womanhood.

The Lady Nanette was not a beauty, though sometimes when she smiled an inner loveliness enchanted those with eyes to see. She had a pleasant, plain face, and a figure which inclined to plumpness from an early age. Her plainness merely served to fuel the flames of her father's dislike, reminding him of the wife who had failed him, and making him despair of ever finding a husband for his eldest daughter.

Then providence, in the guise of His Majesty King Richard III, sent Sir Harold Fitzwilliam to Murran Castle. Stout, balding and in his middle years, Sir Harold was recently widowed when he made the exhausting journey from London. On reaching his destination, he promptly succumbed to the rigours of an ague, brought on by the bitter winds from the sea.

To Nanette fell the task of caring for their sick guest. She had learned the skills from Bethany, and since the old woman's death it was to her that everyone looked when there was sickness in the castle.

Nanette was as kind as she was plain, so perhaps it was not surprising that the ailing knight should fall in love with her. What was perhaps surprising was that Nanette returned his affection.

The match was not a great one: Sir Harold was a man of modest means, twenty years her senior and not particularly intelligent. He spoke hesitantly, was slow to see the point of a jest, but laughed with great gusto when it was made plain to him. The Earl dismissed him as a buffoon, but accepted his offer for the Lady Nanette's hand in marriage without a qualm, and without consulting his daughter.

However, Nanette was eager for the match; perhaps part of her eagerness came from a desire to be her own mistress, but she found her genial knight a comfortable companion and looked for nothing but contentment in her coming marriage. Her one sorrow was that she must leave Elspeth behind.

Now, she looked into her sister's rebellious face and sighed. 'Dearest Elspeth, I know it will be hard for you here when I am gone—but you must work at your studies and control your temper. Perhaps our father will relent and let you come to us in time. Harold has asked that you be allowed to make your home with us . . .'

Elspeth jumped to her feet, her face filled with a blind, hot passion. 'Oh, Nan, do not lie to me! You know father will never relent, because the Countess will not let him. She resents losing your services—no one sews as well as you!—and I am to take your place as her slave.'

Lady Nanette smiled gently. 'I was never that, my dear. It was my duty to attend our stepmother whenever I could be of service to her, naturally.'

'There is nothing natural about it!' cried Elspeth hotly, her face flushed with anger. 'The Lady Margaret has her own waiting women—why should she treat you as though you were a servant? You are the daughter of an earl, while she was a mere nobody before her marriage.'

'Hush, my love, you upset yourself for nothing.' Nan's voice was soothing, and some of the anger died out of Elspeth's face. 'I have borne my lot in patience, as you must. The time will come when you will be free. You will not have to wait long for a husband—you are far too pretty. Harold will prevail upon father to arrange a suitable match for you when the time is right. Harold has some influence with the King.'

Nanette's voice had taken on a note of pride, and Elspeth bit back the scathing retort which sprang to her lips. Not for the world would she hurt her beloved sister by letting her guess the contempt she felt for Sir Harold.

Elspeth could not imagine a worse fate than to be married to such a man. His slow, pompous manner would drive her to distraction within a week!

She turned away, a wistful look in her dark eyes as she said: 'If only I had been a boy, then perhaps father would not have married again.' Suddenly she felt a rush of anger. 'It is not fair! Why should we be treated so scurvily? Jasper and Robert can do no wrong, while we . . .' she broke off with a sob.

Nanette stood up, her long gown sweeping over the stone floor as she moved to take her sister in her arms. 'Do not cry, Elspeth. I love you—and so does poor Nessie, for what that's worth.'

Elspeth gave a strangled laugh. 'Poor Nessie—she is even worse off than we are. It was a black day for her when her husband died and she had to beg our father to take her in.'

'Yes—but a blessed one for us. I could scarcely read or write my name until she came. All I knew was the little our mother taught me before she died. Bethany showed me many things, but she knew nothing of embroidery or keeping accounts.'

Elspeth smiled tenderly. She knew with what difficulty her sister laboured over the long columns of figures she kept for the household accounts. A duty laid on her by her stepmother; because, Elspeth suspected, the Countess could neither read nor write herself. She had never admitted this, and she made a great show of going over the accounts, but she had never questioned the figures. Her forbearance was unusual, for she criticised whenever she could, giving rise to Elspeth's suspicions since her quick brain had often spotted small mistakes in her sister's figures. Sometimes she put them right, but only if she could manage it without Nanette guessing what she had done.

Her temper cooled as quickly as it had flared into life. She kissed Nanette's cheek and released herself from her embrace.

'Oh, do not mind me, Nan. I shall miss you, of course, but I must not be selfish. I am glad you are to be married—no, truly I am.'

Lady Nanette smiled and sat down, taking up her needlework again. 'You will visit us soon, I am sure of it. Father cannot forbid it for ever.'

Elspeth sighed and moved to the window once more, looking out at the courtyard below. It was a hive of activity, with men and horses everywhere.

'I can see him more clearly now. He has dismounted and he is talking to father and Sir Harold. He is taller than father.'

Nanette glanced at her, puzzled. She had forgotten Elspeth's excitement at the arrival of Sir Harold's cousin. 'Of whom are you speaking, my dear?'

'The Wolf of Alvar, of course,' replied Elspeth, a note of impatience in her voice. 'Do you think he is really as wicked as Nessie says? He looks rather handsome from here.'

'Nessie can be very silly sometimes,' said Nanette, a hint of reproof in her voice. 'Lord Alvar cannot possibly be that evil—he is Harold's cousin.'

Elspeth laughed, finding her sister's conviction that Alvar could not be wicked because he was Harold's kinsman irresistibly funny. Her laughter was high and joyous, like church bells on a scented summer's breeze, the sound of it reaching the men in the courtyard below.

The tall stranger, whom Elspeth knew must be Lord Alvar because of his pennant with the wolf's head, looked up as if seeking the source of the laughter. Elspeth was well hidden from his view, but she could see the deep blue of his eyes and his hawklike features quite clearly. She felt a shiver of fear shoot through her. His eyes were hard and cold like a mountain stream in mid-winter. Suddenly she believed all the tales Nessie had told her of men murdered in their beds, and maidens dragged from their fathers' houses to suffer a fate more terrible than death itself.

The times were lawless, heaven knew, with England torn by the warring factions of Lancaster and York. King Richard himself was rumoured to have murdered the young princes in the Tower when he seized the throne after King Edward died. But in an age when the weakness of their rulers allowed the nobles to amass their own private armies, petty quarrels between neighbours often ended in bloodshed. Even so, few men had a reputation to equal that of Alvar. Not for nothing had he chosen the wolf's head as his crest.

Elspeth drew back from the window, chilled by a feeling of imminent disaster. She, who had fearlessly faced a whipping from her father on numerous occasions, was somehow afraid of the man below in the courtyard. Her imagination fired by Nessie's tales, she had been excited by the prospect of his arrival at the castle, but now she was overcome with a sense of dread.

Shivering, she sat down on the stool at her sister's side, unable to voice her fears even to her beloved Nan. Somehow she was sure that her life would never be the same after this day, though she did not know why. But with a sudden wisdom well beyond her years, she knew Nanette's choice of a husband was not after all as foolish as she had believed. There could be worse fates!

The great hall seemed to be full of men, Elspeth thought as she looked down from the gallery. Amongst the guests gathered for the feast on the eve of Lady Nanette's wedding to Sir Harold were no more than a handful of ladies. Just the Countess and her serving women Nessie, and the Earl's own sister, the Lady Ursula.

Elspeth shrank closer to her sister's side as they walked down the wide staircase leading to the hall, sensing that all eyes were upon them. Sir Harold broke off his conversation with another gentleman and came to the foot of the stairs to greet them; his eyes full of pride as they rested on the face of his future bride.

He bent his bulky figure in a surprisingly elegant bow.

'Lady Nanette—Lady Elspeth. May I have the honour of presenting you to my cousin, Lord Alvar?'

Nanette gave him her gentle smile and took his arm, Elspeth trailing reluctantly behind them. The knowledge that for once she was dressed as befitted the daughter of an Earl, in a gown of richly embroidered satin and velvet, gave her no pleasure; though she and Nessie had spent many happy hours in choosing the materials. The bodice was fashioned of cloth of gold, while the flowing skirts and wide sleeves were of the finest crimson. And her thick, dark hair hung like a shining cloud on her shoulders, a cap of gold threads tied beneath her chin.

She stood just behind her sister, listening but not daring to look as Sir Harold introduced his future bride. Then she heard Alvar's reply and her eyes opened wide with surprise. Perhaps she had expected him to snarl like the wolf he was named; but his voice was deep and soft with a lilting sound which was foreign to her ears, his reply courtly and spoken like a gentleman. She could only stare at him, unable to do more than curtsey when Sir Harold drew her forward with a smile.

'And this is my bride's sister, Alvar, the Lady Elspeth.'

'My cousin has spoken of you, lady,' Alvar's words brought her eyes swiftly to his face. 'I see he did not lie—though I scarce believed him until this moment.'

'M-my lord, forgive me,' she whispered, her heart thumping so painfully that she could hardly breathe. 'I do not understand you.'

Alvar smiled; his eyes as bright as the eyes of her father's favourite kestrel when the hood was taken off. 'Why, lady, he told me you were possessed of a rare and perfect beauty—the like of which he had not seen. As yet you are a budding rose, but it will not be long before your petals unfold.'

'Oh . . .' Elspeth gasped, a tide of betraying colour sweeping up her neck and into her cheeks. No one had ever spoken like this to her before. Her father ignored her when she was not being punished; her brothers teased her cruelly, delighting in pulling her long hair, and her stepmother scolded her. Nanette had said she was pretty, but Elspeth had believed she was only being kind; for having no mirror of her own, she had only seen her face as a blurred shape in a polished pewter platter. Lord Alvar's compliments threw her into confusion, adding to her fear of him.

Alvar laughed. He offered her his arm, taking her hand firmly as she hesitated and drawing her away from her sister's protection to stand by the huge, open fireplace. 'Do not look so scared, lady,' he said, a wry smile curving his lips. 'I shall not devour you for my supper. I seek only the privilege of your company.'

Elspeth's pride was stung by what she thought was mockery in his voice. Her eyes flashed and her head shot up. 'I am not frightened of you, sir,' she lied, hiding her trembling hands in the folds of her gown.

She saw a gleam of amusement in his eyes. 'Of course not—why should you be afraid? Even the wolf does not turn on his own. You have nothing to fear from me, lady, believe me.'

Elspeth flushed at his reference to the wolf, which must mean he had guessed her nervousness resulted from listening to the tales told of him. He was staring at her boldly, obviously enjoying her confusion. Suddenly she felt a surge of anger, and with it a return of her courage.

'Wolves are but animals, sir, they hunt by instinct for food. Only a mad beast kills for pleasure.'

Alvar's smile disappeared instantly; his nostrils flared and his lips went white. His hand shot out, gripping her wrist with immensely strong fingers which bit into her flesh, making her wince with pain.

'Be careful, lady,' he warned, his voice grating harshly. 'You know not what you say.'

Elspeth looked up at him, dark eyes meeting blue with

a clash of steel. 'Can you say it is not so, my lord?'

For a moment the fury in his eyes terrified her. She felt her stomach churn and cursed her foolish tongue. What perverse mood possessed her that she must challenge this dangerous man so boldly? Only a simpleton would seek to make an enemy of him. Her brain sought furiously for some means of escape from this terrifying confrontation, finding it at last in her stepmother's frowning countenance.

'Pray excuse me, my lord, I see the Countess wishes me to go to her.'

For an instant his fingers tightened around her wrist as though he would deny her, then he released her with a jerk of his head. 'Go then, lady.'

Elspeth felt relief wash over her as she moved across the room to her stepmother's side. Lord Alvar had been aptly named despite his handsome face and courtly manners, she thought; beneath the surface lay the snarling beast which was his true self. Nessie had been right!

'Have you forgot your manners, girl?' the Countess scolded as Elspeth reached her. 'Here is your Aunt Ursula come for the wedding, and you have not spoke one word to her.'

Elspeth curtsied to her aunt; a tall stately woman with harsh features and a long neck. 'Grant me your forgiveness, aunt. I was delayed in coming to you.'

Ursula inclined her head regally. 'You would do well to avoid delays of that nature in future, Elspeth. That man is no fit companion for a girl of your age.'

Elspeth controlled a spurt of annoyance, schooling her lips into a grateful smile. 'I thank you for your advice, aunt, and I shall take care to heed your warning.' She did not add that she needed no warning as she intended to stay as far away from Lord Alvar as she could!

'You are a good, sensible girl,' her aunt responded approvingly. 'I have been trying to persuade Lady Margaret to let you come back with me. I have no children of my own to bear me company—but she vows she cannot bear to part with you.'

The Countess gave a false laugh. 'What, part with both Nanette and Elspeth in one fell swoop? No, my dear Ursula, you cannot expect it of me. I must have Elspeth to support me after my beloved Nanette has gone. With all the pleasures of London to divert you, you cannot begin to know how I suffer in the long winters . . .'

Ursula smiled, raising her brow. 'You forget that this was my home until I married. I know how tedious life can be, shut up in the castle for weeks on end. Very well, I shall not plague you—but you will have to part with Elspeth one day, you know. And then I shall play my part. The girl is too beautiful to waste on another Sir Harold. I insist upon arranging a suitable match for her when the time comes.'

The Countess frowned. 'The child is too young to be thinking of marriage. You will turn her head, Ursula.'

'I doubt it. Elspeth has too much sense to give way to idle vanity.' She smiled at her niece. 'Your father is pleased with the match between Sir Harold and your sister. I think I might have done better for her—but she is no beauty and it is well enough. However, your marriage is an entirely different matter.'

'It is good of you to concern yourself with my future, aunt, but I would rather not think of taking a husband just yet.'

Ursula frowned. 'It is for you to do as you are told, girl, not to think. Well, well, go to your sister now. She looks for you and we can talk of this another day. I did not come all this way simply to see Nanette wed. I shall stay the month before I leave.'

Elspeth curtsied to her aunt and her stepmother once more, then went thankfully to join her sister. Ursula watched her go, her sharp eyes noting that she was not the only one to follow the girl's progress across the room.

She frowned, turning to Lady Margaret again. 'How old is Elspeth now—sixteen?'

'She is almost fifteen.'

Ursula pursed her lips. 'She looks older. Some girls mature younger than others. Mark my words, when a man like Alvar notices a girl she has ceased to be a child! If I were you, Margaret, I should get her safely wed. A girl as beautiful as that has trouble written all over her . . .'

Fighting her tears, Elspeth responded passionately to her sister's embrace. Sir Harold had granted them a few moments together before carrying off his wife to her new home.

'May God bless you, my dearest,' Nanette whispered, close to tears herself despite her own happiness. 'We must pray that father lets you come to us soon.'

'Oh, Nan,' Elspeth's voice broke on a sob. 'You will write to me sometimes?'

'I will send you word whenever I can,' Lady Nanette promised. 'Do not despair, my sweet sister. I shall remember you always in my prayers.'

'And I shall think of you every moment of every day,' Elspeth vowed. She drew a deep shuddering breath. 'You must go now. You should not keep Sir Harold waiting.'

Nanette held out her hand, and together they went down to the courtyard, where a group of horsemen awaited their coming. Sir Harold had accepted his cousin's offer of an escort on their journey home, knowing that Alvar's protection would assure them of safety no matter who they chanced to meet on the road. Few men would risk attacking the Wolf of Alvar, those who did seldom lived to ponder their error.

Elspeth bade her sister's husband a formal farewell, receiving a brotherly kiss on her cheek and a small parcel thrust into her hands.

At her look of surprise, he flushed, seeming embarrassed. '’Tis a small gift, sister, a token of my affection.'

Elspeth smiled. 'I am sorry to lose my sister, sir, but I believe you will treat her kindly. I wish you both happiness.'

He took her hands, gripping them tightly. 'I thank you for your good wishes, Elspeth. I know Nanette would dearly love to have you with us. Believe me, I will do all I can to persuade your father to relent.'

Elspeth nodded, but she could not bring herself to answer. She clasped her hands behind her back, refusing to betray her misery before the watchful eyes of Alvar. That he was watching her, she was well aware, though she would not catch his eyes. Since their first meeting she had taken care not to let him detach her from her aunt's side. Ursula had mounted guard over her with a relentless vigilance for the past few days. Normally Elspeth would have resented the curtailment of her freedom within the castle walls, but her fear of Alvar was such that she welcomed her aunt's interference. She closed her eyes briefly, blinking back her tears.

'Will you not bid me farewell, lady?'

Alvar's voice made her jump. She spun round, looking anxiously for Lady Ursula's stately figure; but her aunt was standing beside Nanette's palfrey, gazing up at her, and for once she had failed to notice Alvar approach her younger niece.

'I wish you God-speed, sir,' Elspeth said, tilting her chin at him proudly.

Alvar laughed. 'I think you wish me to the devil, lady—but I will not hold it against you. If you were but a year or two older I would carry you hence if I had to kill every man here to do it!'

Elspeth gasped, the colour draining from her cheeks. 'What mean you, sir?'

Alvar's eyes gleamed. 'I mean to have you, lady. I shall return to claim you one day—remember me!' With that he left her, springing on to his horse's back with the agility of a wild cat.

Elspeth pressed her hand against her mouth, willing herself not to give way to the hysteria threatening to overcome her senses.

'I mean to have you, lady.' His words were etched into her brain in letters of fire. 'Remember me,' he had said. How could she ever forget him?

CHAPTER TWO

FROM the narrow windows of her chamber, Elspeth watched the press of men and horses jostling below in the courtyard. It was a scene of confusion and noise, of wailing women from the village reluctant to part with their sweethearts; the rough laughter of the men and stamping hooves; of wagon wheels on cobblestones and the tramp of many feet. Soon her father and his men-at-arms would be leaving the fortress, on their way to join King Richard at Nottingham. Yesterday evening a messenger had reached them as the last rays of a hot August sun had faded from the sky. Almost exhausted, his horse foam-lathered and near dead, the man had fallen on his knees before the Earl.

'My lord, the King demands you join him with all speed, for even now the Usurper is landed at Milford Haven and marches through Wales rousing his supporters!'

The Earl growled low in his throat. 'By thunder! Does the Tudor dog dare to raise his standard against the house of York?' He wheeled round, barking orders at his steward in a sudden fury. 'We march at first light—prepare the men.'

Immediately the castle was thrown into confusion as hasty preparations were made for the arduous march. Elspeth, like everyone else in the Earl's household, was aware of his cold anger. She knew he would respond to the King's summons, not for love of Richard, but out of his hatred for all those who bore the name of Lancaster—even though it be on the wrong side of the blanket.

In the Earl's estimation, Henry Tudor was nought but

the son of an obscure Welsh nobleman and the Plantagenet heiress Lady Margaret Beaufort. The Lady Margaret's grandfather, John of Gaunt's second son by Katherine Swynford, had been born out of wedlock; and though his parents had later wed, and he had been legitimised, he and his heirs had been barred from the succession by attainder. Therefore, Henry Tudor's claim to the throne of England was a tenuous one. Much of the support offered him was because he had promised to wed Elizabeth of York, eldest daughter of King Edward IV; but such promises made little impression on the Earl of Murran.

In him burned the deep-seated hatred of a life-long Yorkist who had too often seen his country torn apart by bloody war as the Red and White Roses struggled for supremacy. For many years now the rival factions of Lancaster and York had warred one against the other, treachery and murder following hard upon the heels of rebellion.

The Earl had seen his father and brothers cut down on the field of battle; and he himself bore the scars of old wounds. He had fought as a young man at St Albans in 1455 when the Wars of the Roses first began. He had suffered bitter defeat at the hands of HenryVI in 1459 when His Majesty subdued the rebellion of the Yorkist lords. He had ridden at Richard of York's side in 1460 when Henry was defeated at Northampton. He had seen Henry deposed the following year and the house of York ascend the throne. Through all the years of unrest which followed, the Earl had supported the White Rose and in his heart had grown this bitter hatred for all those who bore the name of Lancaster. So even though Richard of Gloucester was a monster, who had waded to the throne thigh-deep in blood and infamy, the Earl of Murran would fight at his side. Not from a sense of loyalty to Richard, but because above all else he desired revenge—and he would rather die than see the Tudor upstart rule England!

'Will you not come down and bid your father farewell, child?'

Elspeth turned at the sound of Nessie's voice, moving away from the window. Anger flickered in her dark eyes, and her resemblance to the proud Earl of Murran was very evident as she stared haughtily at her kinswoman.

'Why should I?' she asked, her voice harsh with bitterness. 'Do you think he cares whether I come or not?'

Nessie sighed. Elspeth was every bit as proud and stubborn as her father. Seldom a day passed without a clash of wills between them, and it was not always the Earl who emerged triumphant from the fray. Nessie suspected that he had a secret respect for his wilful daughter, despite all his attempts to crush her spirit. Of late he had ceased to use the whip on her, and though he still demanded total obedience, Elspeth often went unpunished for her sins. However, last night she had pushed him too far and her lovely face still carried the mark of his displeasure in the form of a dark bruise.

'Your father commands your presence,' Nessie said, realising that persuasion would not work. 'I am sent to fetch you—I dare not return without you.'

'Then hide in your chamber until he leaves,' Elspeth retorted waspishly, a pang of remorse striking her as she saw Nessie flinch. 'No, no, I did not mean it. Forgive me, dearest, I spoke hastily. Of course I will come.'

Nessie smiled at her. 'I am sure the Earl did not mean to strike you so hard—you should not have pressed him so sorely when you knew he was in a rage.'

Elspeth's eyes smouldered. 'May the devil take Henry Tudor! If it were not for him I should even now be on my way to Nanette's house.'

Nessie looked at her sympathetically, understanding her moodiness only too easily. It was over a year since the Lady Nanette had wed Sir Harold and in all that time the sisters had not met. The Countess vowed she could not part with Elspeth, and the Earl had withheld his permission for his youngest daughter to visit her sister until a month since. Suddenly he had relented for no apparent reason, and the long-awaited journey had been arranged. Elspeth was to have set out this very morning with an escort of six men-at-arms and Nessie to bear her company; but the Earl had withdrawn his consent last night after the news of the rebellion reached them.

'Your journey must wait, Elspeth,' he had said, summoning her to him. 'You will be needed here since your brothers and I must leave.'

Elspeth stared at him in dismay. 'No! You cannot mean it,' she cried, temper flaring instantly. 'That is unfair, sir, you cannot refuse me now!'

'By thunder! Do you tell me what I may or may not do, daughter?' His eyes darkened with fury, matching her own. 'I march to war with your brothers. We do our duty—will you do less?'

Elspeth flushed. At any other time she would have been proud that in his absence her father considered her presence in the castle a necessity. Now, however, she was too disappointed to think clearly. All the old resentment rose like bile in her throat to choke her. Jasper and Robert were to ride with their father, though she was the elder by two years. But because she was a woman she must remain behind at the beck and call of her stepmother, idling away her days in wearisome tasks which irked her beyond bearing.

'But you promised,' she said angrily, giving no clue to the real reason for her fury. 'Could I not ride with you as far as Nanette's—you need send no escort with me when you turn aside on your journey.'

'Foolish girl, do you think to travel the roads alone? I go to war, Elspeth, not to a tournament. Your place is here with Lady Margaret.'

'Am I to spend all my days as a servant to your wife?' she demanded hotly, all caution gone as she met his furious eyes. 'Do you forget I am as much your flesh as her whelps?'

The Earl's hand shot out, catching Elspeth's cheek with a stinging blow which sent her staggering back. 'No, by God! I do not forget,' he yelled, beside himself with rage. 'This time you have gone too far, daughter. Get you hence before I lose all reason and thrash you as you deserve.'

Elspeth retreated, but not before giving him a darkling glance which left him speechless with fury. Despite his angry look, however, the Earl was secretly proud of his stubborn daughter. Sometimes he found himself wishing she had been the son he had wanted so desperately.

'She's got more spirit in her little finger than Jasper and Robert put together,' he admitted to his steward later that night. 'I vow the wench would ride into battle at my side if I let her!'

'She is your true flesh, my lord,' the steward replied.

'Aye—aye, that she is, and she has my temper, I'll warrant you.' The Earl laughed suddenly. 'She will hate me for it, Carson, but I'll rest easier knowing she is here.'

Carson nodded. 'With the men we shall still have we could withstand a siege for several weeks, my lord, providing the men stayed loyal.'

'Aye.' The Earl smiled grimly. 'There is not a man in the castle who would not fight for Elspeth to his last drop of blood.'

Carson hesitated, then: 'Perhaps if you explained to the Lady Elspeth . . . ?' he said, waiting for the storm to burst over his head; but the Earl merely shrugged.

'She will do as I tell her—I will be obeyed!'

The steward abandoned the argument. It was useless to say more. The Earl had good reason for refusing to allow his daughter to leave the castle: in his absence his enemies might seize the chance to settle old scores—and there was always the danger of a raid from across the border. The Earl's men were all fiercely loyal to their lord and the Lady Elspeth, though few of them had much love for the Countess. She was a coarse woman with a scolding tongue who did not inspire devotion. Elspeth, however, had a rare charm which combined with her beauty to bind a spell over those who served her. Despite her tempers, there was a basic sweetness in her nature which drew others to her. At sixteen she was the kind of woman some men would want to write sonnets for, while others would spill blood to win her favours.

As yet Elspeth was unaware of her own power. Living in the shadow of her half-brothers, she had learned only to despise herself for being a woman. Perhaps if her father had explained why she was needed in the castle she might not so bitterly resent the curtailed visit to her sister, but he did not. He had never considered anyone else's feelings in his life, and he did not know how to reach his fiery daughter.

When she appeared in answer to his summons, shortly before he was ready to leave the castle, he greeted her coldly. 'Remember your duty, Elspeth,' he growled, his face hard. 'Let none enter who have no right within the castle walls. Have a care for Lady Margaret—and see that you learn better manners before I return!'

Elspeth met his unyielding gaze, some of her anger melting queerly into a repressed agony. Suddenly she understood that her father was going to war and might never return. It was a blinding flash of pain, striking at her heart. She stared at him helplessly, knowing she loved him despite the years of neglect, wanting to tell him so and failing to find the words.

She clenched her hands into tight fists, suppressing a desire to weep. 'I will do my duty, father. God keep you.'

The Earl regarded her in silence. Perhaps in that moment he came as close to recognising his love for her as it was possible for him to do. 'God be with you, Elspeth,' he said, hesitating as he was seized by a desire to clasp her in his arms before he left. He took two steps towards her and stopped, ashamed of his moment of weakness. Turning abruptly, he strode away, leaving her staring after him.

It was more than a month now since her father had ridden out at the head of his men. August had turned into September, and sometimes a cold mist floated in from the sea, warning that autumn was on its way. Elspeth sighed, moving away from her window. As far as the eye could see the landscape was empty, except for a hawk soaring above in the sky and a strange wisp of smoke from the direction of the village, which was hidden from her view by a steep bank. A pall of silence seemed to hang over the castle, heavy, brooding, like the unnatural lull before a storm.

Elspeth knew the tension was spreading through the rest of the household: some thirty men-at-arms, a sprinkling of women servants, a page boy and Carson. These few had remained behind to defend the castle while the others marched in the Earl's train to join King Richard. Thirty soldiers, a boy and an old man where there was normally a garrison of some three hundred fighting men besides the servants and the villagers. Perhaps it was hardly surprising that the castle should seem empty, yet the tension had built slowly this past week.

Part of Elspeth's anxiety was because there had been no word from the Earl. True it was many miles from here to Nottingham, but her father would lose no time in sending news of a victory. There should have been some word, Elspeth thought for the hundredth time that day. News of a battle at least, if not a victory. Something—anything!—to ease the gnawing anxiety felt by everyone in the castle.

'Your stepmother is asking for you, Elspeth.'

At the sound of Nessie's voice, Elspeth spun round,

her face lighting up. 'Is there news?' she asked. 'Has a messenger come?'

Nessie shook her head regretfully. 'No—there is no message, my dear. The Countess is fretful. She would have you play your lute for her—she says the music will soothe her nerves.'

Elspeth frowned. She would have liked to refuse her stepmother's request, but she knew the Countess was as anxious as everyone else—and she had promised her father to do her duty by his wife.

'Very well, Nessie, I will come . . .' she began, breaking off as she heard shouting in the courtyard. Rushing to her window, she waited only to see that the cause of the excitement was a man dressed in the simple garb of a villager. 'I must go down,' she cried, a mixture of fear and anticipation churning in her stomach. 'At last there is some word from my father!'

Dodging past Nessie, she ran out of the room, gathering up her trailing skirts as she hurried down the sharply curving steps of the tower. Reaching the great hall, she saw her father's steward, his lined, careworn face creased with anxiety. He called to her:

'Grave news, my lady.'

Elspeth halted, the colour draining from her face. 'Bad news?' she whispered, her heart thudding painfully. 'Is—is my father dead?'

Carson blinked at her stupidly for a moment, then shook his head. 'Nay, my lady, there is no word from the Earl as yet. 'Tis from the village—this morning before 'twas light a party of Scots raided the cattle. They burned three cottages and six are dead.'

'Dead? Six are dead?' Elspeth opened her eyes wide in horror. 'But . . . there were only women, children and old men left to tend the crops . . . the young men went with my father . . .'

Carson nodded, his eyes reflecting the resignation of an old man who had seen too much of the world to be surprised at any new atrocity perpetrated by man on his fellow creatures. 'Aye, my lady. Women, children and sick, old men. No match for those murdering devils from across the border.'

Hot, burning anger flared in Elspeth, so bitter that it was as gall in her throat. 'They must have chosen to strike now while my father is away, believing we are too weak to retaliate.'

'Yes,' Carson agreed sadly. 'We dare not send a force against them—we cannot spare the men.'

Elspeth frowned impatiently; already a plan was forming in her brain. 'I want to see the villager who brought the news—fetch him to me. I would learn more of these brave warriors who attack women and children.'

The steward hesitated. 'Is it wise, my lady?' he asked, sensing trouble as he saw the storm clouds brewing in her lovely face. 'We cannot send a force after them.'

Elspeth stamped her foot. 'Stop whining like a wounded cur,' she snapped. 'We have thirty men—we can spare half to bring these beasts to heel. They will not be expecting us to go after them, therefore we shall have the advantage of a surprise attack.'

Carson's mouth fell open. 'You do not mean to—my lady!—you cannot do it!'

Elspeth's face hardened, never had she looked more like her father. 'Do you dare to tell me what I cannot do?' she demanded, her eyes flashing furiously. 'Fetch the messenger to me. I will question him myself. Then tell the men to prepare to leave, but to await my orders. I shall need a horse—and a man's saddle.'

Carson started to protest, but a flash from her dark eyes silenced him, knowing that she was too much the Earl's daughter to listen to saner counsel once her blood was roused. He hurried away to carry out her orders, muttering to himself and trying not to think of the Earl's fury if he should learn of this day's work. Minutes later, he returned with the villager in tow.

The man hobbled painfully behind him, dragging the lame leg which had kept him from marching with the

Earl. He dropped to his knees before Elspeth, bowing his head as if afraid to look at her.

'Get up, good sir,' Elspeth said, her voice gentle now. 'I would hear for myself what you have to say.'

He rose to his feet, meeting her gaze awkwardly. ''Twas this way, my lady,' he said. ''Twas first light when they came yelling and hollering into the village like all the devils in hell. Wild they were—huge men, as huge as giants, with hairy faces and eyes that glowed green in the firelight. First they drove off the cattle, then they set fire to Widow Pearson's cottage. They dragged her out by her hair and . . .' he broke off as he remembered to whom he was speaking. 'Some of the lads tried to stop them, my lady, and they cut them down. They killed my brother's only son. I saw it with my own eyes. The boy was but eight summers—what will I tell Seth when he returns . . .' his voice broke on a sob.

'How many were there?' Elspeth asked, ignoring his last question because she dare not let pity cloud her judgment. He blinked at her foolishly and she sighed with impatience. 'All right—were there as many as the fingers on both your hands?'

He looked at his hands wonderingly, then nodded, eager to please her. 'Yes, my lady, they were everywhere—hundreds of them!'

Elspeth frowned. Obviously the man had no idea how to reckon numbers, and she did not believe his description of the raiders; but she knew from listening to her father in the past that the raiding parties were seldom more than a score of men. Her plan was risky: she would have to divide the castle's force in half. Fifteen must remain to guard the castle; the others would ride out with her to track down and punish the raiders.

She questioned the man further, gaining an idea of the route the Scots had taken on their return journey across the border. Then she whirled around and raced back to her solar. Less than twenty minutes later, she was dressed in some of Jasper's discarded clothing and standing in the courtyard, having left Nessie bewildered and weeping in her chamber.

The men-at-arms were gathered in the inner bailey, awaiting her orders. They stared at her as she appeared in youth's clothing, their faces registering various degrees of astonishment.

'Well?' she demanded. 'What are we waiting for? One of you must help me mount— For mercy's sake! Why do you stare so? Will you obey me or not?'

One of them, a thick-set, bearded man named Firkin, laughed suddenly, his eyes glowing with amusement and admiration. 'Aye, I'll follow you, my lady—to hell and back if you command it—and so will we all!'

There was a murmur of approval from the others, and then a burst of activity as they swung into action. Firkin offered his hand to Elspeth, tossing her up into the saddle easily.

Elspeth was no stranger to boy's attire, nor was this the first time she had ridden astride like a man. As a child she had been whipped on a score of occasions for sneaking out to the stables in her brother's clothing—and those were the times she was unlucky enough to get caught. Often the grooms or one of the pages covered her escape, for none of the servants would willing betray her to the Earl. However, Elspeth had given up the masquerade once her womanly curves could no longer be hidden. But today she wore a cloak draped over her velvet tunic and hose, and her long hair was covered by a close-fitting hood. To the casual observer she would pass for a youth.

Digging her heels in sharply, Elspeth urged her horse forward, leading the way through the outer courtyard and across the drawbridge, which was pulled up after them. She did not look back as she heard the heavy clang, even though her heart was racing wildly. If she was to hold the respect of her men, Elspeth knew she must show no sign of fear.

At this moment she found that easy enough, for her

only emotions were excitement and a sense of release. This was the adventure she had craved for so long! Anger had spurred her on at the start, but simply to have sent her men in pursuit should have cooled her desire for revenge. As she urged her horse ever faster, Elspeth knew it was boredom and frustration which had sent her on this mad venture. For mad it most certainly was! She had not needed Nessie to tell her that. But she would not allow herself to think of her stepmother's scolding tongue—nor her father's fury when he returned!

Because the raiders had been so confident that no retaliation would be launched against them, they had not bothered to hide their tracks, leaving a trail of trampled crops and flattened grass. Nor had they scurried back across the border as was their usual practice.

Besides the cattle, they had carried off two maidens from the village and several casks of ale. When the pursuing soldiers caught up with them, they had already made camp for the night, despite the fact that there were still several hours of daylight left. No sentries had been posted: the reason for this soon became clear as the sound of drunken laughter and a girl's terrified screams floated out on the air.

On the brow of a rise, some distance from the raiders' camp, the soldiers halted, deciding to leave their horses and continue on foot, thus surprising the drunken Scots.

Firkin frowned, turning to Elspeth he said: 'You had best wait here, my lady. It will not be a pretty sight.'

Elspeth bit back a sharp retort. She had tended too many wounded men to faint at the sight of blood; but though she would have fought at their side if she could, she knew she would only hinder them.

'I will watch the horses,' she said, keeping her voice low. 'God be with you all.'

Firkin looked at her, his eyes hard. 'Shall we take prisoners, my lady?'

Elspeth shook her head. 'No,' she said, her face pale

but determined. 'They are vile murderers—give no quarter.'

In that moment she was more the Earl of Murran's child than she had ever been. One by one the soldiers filed past her, saluting her silently, their swords pressed flat against their lips as if consecrating a solemn oath.

Quietly, relentlessly, the Earl's men crept through the gathering dusk, taking care not to warn their quarry of their approach. The Scots never knew what was happening until it was too late. Intent on their sport with the village girls, they failed to hear the stealthy rustling of bracken beneath the soldiers' feet. Before they realised they were being attacked, half of them had been hacked to pieces by the cruel, flashing broadswords. Those that recovered their wits enough to make a fight of it were too drunk to stand a chance against the vengeful soldiers. Some of them tried to run; they were cut down from behind. Others pleaded for mercy on their knees, but they begged in vain—there was no mercy that night.

From the brow of the hill, Elspeth watched the bloody carnage in the flare of the camp fire. Her body rigid with shock, she clasped her hands over her ears to shut out the terrible screams of dying men as she saw the havoc she had wrought. Suddenly she doubled over and vomited behind a thorn bush, wiping her mouth on her sleeve as the ground swayed momentarily beneath her feet.

'Oh God, I did not know,' she whispered, her eyes dark with horror. 'Forgive me—I did not know . . .'

She had longed for vengeance against the raiders with all her heart, but not once had she stopped to think what it would mean. It was easy to condemn one's enemies to death, but not so easy to watch the results in cold blood. A life for a life, that was the motto by which her father lived. If he had been here he would have acted just as she had, this she knew. But that did not make it right. Now she was as guilty as those wretched Scots down there. She had blood on her hands!

Alone and trembling in the darkness, Elspeth waited for the soldiers' return. All fifteen came back, their faces savage with triumph as they wiped the blood from their swords on the grass. Not one of them had received more than a trivial flesh wound. They were shouting and laughing, their voices high with glee as they exchanged stories of bloody deeds.

'The raiders are all dead, my lady,' said Firkin. 'The Scots will think twice before they burn our villages again.'

Elspeth could not bring herself to meet his eyes. 'You have done well,' she said, forcing herself to speak calmly. She must remember the dead women and children! The raiders had shown no mercy—they deserved their fate! She must hold on to that and shut out the screams of dying men.

The two girls who had been captured by the Scots were sobbing wildly. One of them flung herself at Elspeth, sinking to the ground at her feet and clasping her around the knees.

'Oh, blessed lady,' she sobbed. 'May God reward you in Heaven for saving us.'

Elspeth touched her head, a renewed sense of anger driving memories of the Scots' screams to a far corner of her mind. 'Get up, child,' she said. 'You are safe now—thanks to these brave men.'

The girl seized her hand and kissed it. 'You led them here, my lady. I heard them talking—they say it was because of you that good fortune rode with them today. They are calling you an angel . . .'

Elspeth suddenly realised that all eyes were upon her: it was time to put away her conscience and resume the responsibilities she had assumed so gaily just a few, short hours ago.

'We must return to the castle,' she said. 'See—the moon comes up to light our way. Two of you take up the women before you—five of you must drive the cattle while the rest ride with me.'

The men moved instantly to obey her. Elspeth was aware of their eyes following her as she mounted her horse. They believed she had brought them good luck; for the Scots had outnumbered them, and had the circumstances been other than they were, the Earl's men might even now be dead or dying. Hardened soldiers they might be, but a streak of superstition bound them by a common thread. When they set out on their mission earlier they had followed her because she was the Earl's daughter, now she had become a kind of talisman to them.

The other woman had been taken up, and the cattle were being herded. Now the soldiers closed their ranks about her, turning once more in the direction they had come earlier, Elspeth riding at their head as they sped through the night. Yet even now their luck held good, for the sky was lit with a silver glow which made their journey easier.

Somewhere a night owl hooted as it swooped down on its unsuspecting prey. Elspeth heard the pain-filled scream of a terrified creature as the cruel talons pierced its flesh. She shivered, memories stirring which she would prefer to forget. But the men who rode with her did not share her mood, nor her premonition of impending disaster. Yet with each mile they covered the feeling that everything had gone too well grew within her. She listened to the soldiers laughing and jesting with each other, wishing she could share their high spirits. Now the castle walls loomed up out of the rocky ground before them, its towers stark against the silver sky. As if of one mind, men and horses surged forward with renewed speed.

Soon they would be home: sleep, food and the congratulations of their comrades awaited them. Reining to a halt before the moat, Firkin cried in a loud voice: 'Open for the Lady Elspeth! We are returned and all is well.'

There was a brief pause, then the bridge came down

with a resounding clatter which shattered the eerie silence hanging over the castle.

They rode across the bridge, shouting and calling to their comrades jubilantly, but there were no answering shouts. The outer courtyard was strangely empty. No grooms came running to take their horses, no greetings from the Earl's men left behind to guard the castle. As the last soldier crossed the bridge the portcullis clanged down behind him with an ominous thud. The soldiers began to look about them uneasily, suddenly aware that something was not right. Then figures began to emerge from the shadows; they came swiftly, surrounding the riders, preventing the horses from moving on, outnumbering the Earl's men by three to one.

Firkin gave a cry of alarm. 'By God! We've been tricked,' he growled. 'Where are our men?'

A low rumbling swept through the returning soldiers, their hands creeping to the swords they had used to such devastating effect earlier. Moving closer to Elspeth as if of one accord, their horses jostling nervously as the press of strangers closed in about them.

Elspeth stared down into the sea of faces surrounding her. 'Who are you?' she asked, her voice haughty. 'Do you dare to impede the Earl of Murran's daughter?'

'Shall we fight, my lady?' Firkin asked. 'We are mounted—they are on foot . . .'

'That would be most unwise.' A voice spoke from somewhere in the darkness, and the men-at-arms surrounding Elspeth parted to let the speaker through. 'Tell your men to surrender, lady. The castle is already in my hands and the Countess of Murran is my prisoner.'

Elspeth looked down into the cold blue eyes she remembered so well and a shiver of pure terror ran through her. 'Alvar . . .' she whispered. 'Why are you here?'

CHAPTER THREE

For a moment an icy flame flickered in Alvar's eyes, searing Elspeth to the core, making her shudder as she remembered the threat he had made the last time they met.

'Get down, lady,' he commanded, his voice harsh. 'And tell your men to surrender. If they disperse quietly no harm will come to anyone—if they resist they will die.'

Staring down into his hard face, Elspeth hesitated. Wild thoughts of defying him formed in her head. She knew her men were ready to fight to the death for her, and there was a chance that they could force a way through the press of Alvar's soldiers. They might be able to escape through the postern gate; but even as the plan took shape in her mind, she dismissed it. Too many would die in the attempt—besides, she could not escape while the Countess and Nessie remained in Alvar's hands.

She turned to Firkin, keeping her voice steady as she said: 'Dismiss your men, sir. I will have no bloodshed on my account.'

She swung herself from the saddle, shivering as she felt Alvar's hands encircle her waist as he helped her down. She turned to face him, lifting her chin proudly.

Alvar met her challenging look, no hint of softness or pity in his eyes as he said: 'I have come from His Majesty King Henry VII. I have been ordered to tell you that the traitor Murran's lands are forfeit and now rightfully the property of the crown.'

Elspeth's eyes flashed with anger. 'You mean the Earl

of Murran's lands! Do you think my father will stand by and see you strip him of his birthright?'

Elspeth felt a chill enter her heart as she waited defiantly for his answer. Henry Tudor was king, therefore Richard was defeated—and her father! Where was her father now, she wondered fearfully. A prisoner in some isolated fortress, condemned to a traitor's shameful death—or was he already dead?

'The Earl of Murran died on the field of Bosworth.' Did Alvar's hard face soften a little as he broke the news, or was it only Elspeth's imagination? 'Your father died bravely, lady, though not at my hand. He neither gave nor asked for quarter.'

Elspeth felt the pain twist in her like the thrust of a sword. Holding back her tears, she raised her eyes to his. 'And my brothers—what of my brothers, sir?'

'Your brothers were not harmed,' Alvar replied, his voice emotionless. 'They are the King's wards.'

'Then Jasper is now the Earl of Murran. The castle and lands are his by right.'

Alvar's face hardened again. 'That right was forfeited when your father chose to fight against the King. Henry Tudor is master in England now and it is by his order that I am here. I am to leave a garrison of men loyal to Henry in the castle—then we return to London, lady.'

Elspeth's heart jolted with sudden fear. 'We . . . ?' she whispered. 'You mean I am to go with you?'

'I am commanded to bring you to Henry's court. You are to be the King's ward. He wants all the traitor's brood under his eyes—so that you do not hatch another rebellion.'

Elspeth's head shot up proudly, her eyes clashing with his. 'I would rather die than be Henry Tudor's prisoner. You will never get me to London alive. I will escape or perish in the attempt!'

Alvar smiled oddly. 'How fierce you are,' he said, and there was unwilling admiration in his voice. 'But will you condemn your brothers to death?'

Elspeth gasped. 'What do you mean?' she asked, a tingle of horror running through her.

'If you do not obey the King's commands your brothers will pay with their lives.'

'Even Henry Tudor could not be so cruel,' she whispered, her throat dry with fear. 'He could not!'

Alvar's mouth drew into a thin line. 'What has this to do with Henry Tudor? If you defy me I shall kill them both myself.'

Elspeth swayed, the world rocking beneath her feet as she looked up at him. Alvar was a cold, ruthless man, capable of any treachery if the tales told of him were true. At this moment she would gladly have surrendered her own life rather than bow the knee to her father's enemies, but she could not go to her grave with her brothers' deaths on her soul.

She closed her eyes, fighting the sick misery inside her, temporarily defeated; too weary with the long ride and her grief to resist him any more. 'Very well,' she said. 'I will go with you, sir. Now, I beg you, give me leave to retire to my solar.'

The blue eyes flickered over her. 'I believe you set out in pursuit of a band of raiders—did you catch them?'

Elspeth looked at him then, and he saw that her eyes were dark with pain. 'Yes. I was a fool to split my forces—had I been here you would not so easily have gained entry, Lord Alvar.'

Alvar smiled oddly. 'Your mistake was to let your heart rule your head. Your action was brave but unwise.'

Stung to anger by his words, Elspeth's eyes sparkled dangerously. 'I thank you for your advice, sir. You may be sure I shall remember it in future!'

Satisfied with the results of his deliberate goading, Alvar threw back his head and laughed. 'Then I shall watch my back, little she-wolf, lest you sink your fangs into me unawares.'

Alone in her chamber, Elspeth could no longer hold

back her tears. Lying on her narrow chest bed, with its hard mattress of close-packed straw, she let the misery and grief wash over her, engulfed in a tide of despair which threatened to drag her under. She was tired and her body ached from the long ride. She longed for the ministrations of the little serving girl who waited on her, but Alvar had decreed that she could see no one. At this very moment one of his men was on guard outside her door.

As if she would attempt to escape now! He had made sure she could not!

Somehow it made her pain easier to bear when she focused her hatred on Alvar. Then she was able to shut out the memory of her last meeting with her father, but she could not quite smother her feeling of regret. If only she had found the words to tell him of her love. Hot, scalding tears filled her eyes, spilling out in a flood of anguish. And mixed with her grief was a feeling of guilt because she had allowed her father's enemies to seize Jasper's birthright.

Alone in the darkness, without even a taper to light the gloom, Elspeth faced the future. She was Alvar's prisoner. He was taking her to a life of confinement, locked away in a tower, never again to see her loved ones. For a moment she wished that she had died tonight before she learnt of her father's death. Was this God's punishment for the havoc she had wreaked today? A life for a life. According to her father's principles she had acted justly, saving the lives of two village girls. But had anyone the right to take life—was it just to strike out in revenge?

Elspeth sighed. She was barely sixteen, exhausted and worn out with weeping. Such complex problems were beyond her judgment. She only knew that she was alone and frightened. She wished Nessie had been allowed to come to her, but Alvar seemed determined to punish her by forcing her to be alone with her own thoughts.

Gradually the horrors of the day faded from her mind

as weariness overcame her and she slipped into the blessed relief of sleep. She slept soundly, physical exhaustion overriding the tortuous dreams which made her cry out and toss wildly on her cot. But she did not wake when the door of her chamber opened and a black shadow moved silently towards her bed.

A shaft of moonlight through the narrow window illuminated the man's hard face. For a long time he stood watching the sleeping girl, frowning slightly as he saw the tear stains on her cheeks and heard her feverish mutterings. Then he stooped to cover her with the blanket which had slipped away, revealing her slender white body, before walking from the room and locking the door behind him.

In the morning the sunbeams were streaming in through the slitted windows of the tower as Elspeth awoke to see a little serving girl enter bearing a pitcher of water.

Elspeth lept from her bed eagerly, relieved to see a friendly face at last. 'Oh, Meta,' she cried. 'I thought I was to be shut away for ever! What news of Lady Margaret and Nessie? Were many killed in the fighting yesterday? Tell me, how long did it take Alvar's men to bridge our defences?'

The girl stared at her in obvious surprise. 'Why, my lady, there was no fighting. The Countess surrendered to Alvar's men at once.'

Elspeth's face registered her disbelief and shock. 'She gave in without a fight . . .'

'Aye, my lady. Lord Alvar granted her the freedom of the castle and a pardon from His Majesty if she submitted to him immediately. She dined with him last night in the hall.'

Anger stirred in Elspeth, making her want to strike out at someone in her pain and grief. 'The Countess dined with Alvar! How could she? How could she honour her husband's enemy when the Earl is hardly cold in his grave? She has betrayed his memory!'

Meta shuffled her feet awkwardly, wishing she had not spoken. 'I'm sorry, my lady,' she mumbled, not daring to look at her mistress. 'Will you dress now and come down? Lord Alvar wishes to speak with you.'

Elspeth glared at her, controlling the urge to shake the stupid wench. Her first thought was to tell Meta to send Alvar to the devil and refuse to go down; but the alternative was to remain a prisoner in her chamber, and since no food had been sent to her she was likely to starve before Alvar relented. He would deal harshly with any disobedience, of that she was sure. She was not afraid of him for her own sake, but his devious mind would think up some plan to force her to his will. In a glowering silence she allowed Meta to help her into a flowing gown of black velvet. Her thick, dark hair was coiled sleekly on her head, and hidden beneath a close-fitting cap. She tapped her foot impatiently as Meta fastened a girdle of gold threads around her waist and helped her don a loose mantle of heavy silk, fastened at the throat with a knot of coiled gold.

Elspeth had no mirror in which to see herself, and so she had no idea of her own beauty. She was unaware of the regal picture she made as she swept downstairs to the hall below.

Alvar watched her approach, his face expressionless. Another man might have betrayed the storm of emotion she aroused in him, but he gave no sign that he was startled by her beauty. He had remembered her as a tempestuous child with a wild, almost ethereal loveliness; now she stood before him in all the splendour of her youthful beauty, like a butterfly newly emerged from its chrysalis.

His eyes followed the proud tilt of her chin, lingering hungrily on the soft curve of her mouth. Her skin had the bloom of a freshly-opened rose; her glowing eyes were dark pools of mystery he could not fathom. She awoke in him half-forgotten echoes of what he had once been, stirring the ashes of hopes and desires long dead. He wanted her so badly at that moment that his loins ached to feel her softness melting beneath him, and he knew he would know no peace until he possessed her body and soul.

Perhaps a little of what he felt broke through his mask of indifference, or perhaps Elspeth sensed the tension in him. She shivered suddenly, feeling that she was in terrible danger. Instinctively she lowered her long lashes, veiling her fear.

She curtsied to him, summoning every effort of will to appear unconcerned. 'You wished to see me, my lord?'

Alvar relaxed as anger cooled the heat of his desire. Almost two years ago he had respectfully asked the Earl of Murran for his daughter Elspeth's hand in marriage. The Earl had coldly refused his permission, giving no reason for his decision—nor had Alvar asked for one, knowing in his heart that he had had no right to make the request. He had sworn then that he would have her one day, but not as his wife! Since then he had nursed bitter thoughts of wresting her from her father's protection, never dreaming that when he eventually came for her he would be bound by an oath he could not break. She was Henry Tudor's ward—and he was Henry's vassal. He had taken an oath of allegiance which bound him to his Sovereign's service. He laughed suddenly: Elspeth was his prisoner yet she was out of his reach more surely than if a hundred armed men stood between them.

Elspeth looked at him uncertainly. 'Why do you laugh? Do I amuse you?'

Alvar shook his head. 'I was laughing at myself.' He held out his hand to her, in full control of himself once more. 'Come—I know you have not eaten for many hours. You must break your fast before we leave.'

'Leave?' Elspeth's eyes opened wide, a shaft of fear piercing her. 'Do we leave today?'

He smiled strangely, a hint of self-mockery in his eyes. 'I think we must—it would not be wise to tarry overlong. Tell me, do you think you can be ready in three hours?'

Elspeth hung back, clasping her trembling hands beneath her mantle so that he should not guess the panic his words had roused in her. 'I doubt the maids can pack my clothes in so short a time, sir. Can we not delay the journey for at least one day?'

'And give you time to hatch schemes and plots for escape?' Alvar's brows rose. 'Nay, I think not. Your servants have been working since first light. We will take what we can with us, the rest of your belongings can follow later.'

Elspeth felt a sick curdling in her stomach. She did not trust this man. Every nerve in her body cried out against him, warning her to resist the charm of his soft voice and handsome face. She preferred it when he was angry with her, then she could hate him as she ought.

'Then may I take Nessie with me? I pray you, sir, grant me this boon. Do not wrench me from my home so cruelly, allow me this one comfort, I beg you.'

Alvar frowned as if wondering what new mischief she was hatching, then he inclined his head. 'Very well, you may take the woman with you—but remember I shall be watching you always. If you try to escape me I shall carry out my threat.'

Elspeth raised her eyes to his scornfully. 'I am not like to forget, sir. What bitter gall festers in your heart that you must always seek to destroy?'

Alvar's eyes narrowed to thin, blue slits. 'Be careful, lady,' he warned between tightly clenched teeth. 'You tread treacherous ground. Never seek to pry into what does not concern you—or you may learn to regret it!'

They had reached the small chamber at the rear of the hall. There, Elspeth saw, a table had been laid with cold meat, bread and ale. Alvar halted. 'I will leave you to your meal—while I make certain there is no cause for delay. Remember, lady, you must be ready to travel within three hours—so make what adieus you will.' With that he strode away from her, leaving her staring after him in dismay.

Elspeth sat down with a bump. She had few farewells to make, for it would give her no pain to part with her stepmother and Nessie was to come with her. She shivered, frightened by the prospect of leaving all she had ever known.

A servant came to fill her cup. She gave him a preoccupied smile, forcing herself to eat and drink, though the food stuck in her throat. After a few minutes she became aware that the servant was hovering around her, fussing unnecessarily with the jug of ale. The next moment he had knocked it flying, and in the confusion he bent to whisper in her ear.

'Firkin is waiting in the chapel for you.'

Elspeth gave him a startled look, but was wise enough not to reply. There were too many niches in the thick walls where Alvar's servants could spy on them. The message was obviously meant to be a secret, and could bring swift retribution on the messenger's head.

Elspeth finished her ale and pushed away the remains of her meal. Standing up she walked unhurriedly from the room, making her way through the hall and out into the cool September air. She crossed the inner courtyard at the same slow pace, going beneath a carved stone porch into the gloom of the chapel.

Ignoring the high, vaulted roof and the rows of embroidered banners waving proudly from the wooden spans above, she went on down the short aisle and knelt before the altar, bowing her head in prayer.

'Do not look up, my lady.' Firkin's voice reached her in a hushed whisper from behind a curtained recess to her left. 'Continue as if in prayer in case we are watched.'

Elspeth inclined her head slightly, her lips moving as if reciting a prayer.

'Last night I managed to send a message to the men we left behind with the stolen cattle. They are waiting in the woods two miles past the village. At a command from you they will attack Alvar's men as you pass through the woods.'

'Five men can do nothing against Alvar. They would die for nothing.'

'Alvar will have but a dozen men—the others are to remain in the castle. Last night he gave us all the chance to swear an oath of fealty to King Henry. To those who were willing he granted the freedom of the castle and the opportunity to serve him. I shall be one of the men who ride with you, my lady. If I were to kill him first the others would have no heart for the fight.'

'No, it is too risky.' Elspeth crossed herself and stood up. 'I know you mean well, but I forbid you to carry out your plan. If anything should go wrong Alvar has sworn to murder both my brothers.'

'But, my lady . . .'

Elspeth's eyes flashed, warning him to be silent. 'No more of this, sir! One day we shall take our revenge, be assured of that. Watch and wait. Give lip service to Alvar and bide your time. When it is safe to strike I will tell you.'

Firkin bent the knee before her, drawing aside the heavy curtain slightly. 'It shall be as you command, my lady.'

Elspeth nodded and turned to leave the chapel. She had no reason to glance up, and so she did not see the dark figure half hidden in the shadows of a small gallery overlooking the altar. Nor could she have guessed that Alvar had been a silent witness to her meeting with the soldier.

Long before Elspeth left Murran Castle under Alvar's stern protection, Henry Tudor was on his way to the Capital.

After his victory on the field of Bosworth, Henry's first act was to convey the young Earl of Warwick from his prison at Sheriff Hutton in Yorkshire to the Tower of London. This was most likely because he feared the young Earl's claim to the English throne was stronger than his own. At the same time he had another prisoner at Sheriff Hutton taken to London with all due pomp and ceremony. This person was the Princess Elizabeth whom he had pledged himself to marry when he came to power.

Elizabeth was lodged at her mother's house while Henry proceeded to make his triumphant journey to London. He was greeted everywhere as a deliverer, the common people coming out of their homes to acknowledge him as their rightful king. Richard III had been an unpopular monarch, and, as is the way with all beginnings, the people hoped for much from their new master.

However, the crowds lining the streets of London were disappointed that the new king did not ride into the city at the head of his nobles. Instead he chose to hide himself away in a cumbersome carriage, giving rise to the rumour that he was afraid to be seen. Perhaps the truth was that Henry was a more reserved man than they had believed. Destiny had made him a king, but at heart he would always remain a rather careful, parsimonious country gentleman.

The journey from Murran Castle was slow and tedious. The inns at which they stayed were often uncomfortable and ill-kept, their parlours crowded with sweating, unwashed bodies, and smelling of burning fat as the meat roasted over an open fire. Sometimes there was a smaller room where Elspeth could dine with Nessie alone, but often she was forced to eat her supper under the curious eyes of other travellers because Alvar was determined to keep her near him.

'He means to make certain I cannot escape,' Elspeth complained bitterly to Nessie when they had been several days on the road. 'His servants watch me like hawks following the flight of a sparrow. They are never more than a few feet away from me—and even when I sleep one remains outside my door! I am so obviously his prisoner—'tis no wonder folk stare at me so!'

Nessie thought privately that it was the girl's beauty which drew so many curious stares, but she murmured sympathetic agreement. She was not so much concerned at Alvar's keeping a close watch over her kinswoman as at what he might do!

During the last years of her ill-fated marriage she and her husband had lived near the estate of a certain Baron Reinwold Cassell. So she had learned at first-hand of the terrible night when Alvar descended on Cassell Manor with a force of some fifty men-at-arms. By morning the Baron was dead, his house burned to the ground and his young wife had disappeared. Some said she had taken her own life after being dishonoured, others whispered that Alvar had carried her off with him never to be heard of again.

Whatever had happened to the unfortunate woman, it was certain that her husband had been foully murdered and her home destroyed. If Alvar had been capable of such wickedness when he had barely attained his manhood—what was he capable of now?

Nessie was overcome with terror every time he looked their way, not for herself but for Elspeth's sake. Every night she lay down beside the girl in the bed they shared with a small knife hidden beneath her pillow. She was not sure what she would do if the worst happened, but she meant to defend her kinswoman's honour with her life.

So far, however, Alvar had behaved with great restraint during their journey. He was coldly polite, hiding his thoughts behind a mask of stern indifference. Little did Nessie guess that Alvar's guards slept outside Elspeth's room as much to protect the girl as to prevent her escape. Alvar found himself more affected by his beautiful prisoner than he cared to admit. Sometimes he toyed with the idea of carrying her off to his own home in disobedience of the King's orders. Flanked on two sides by the sea and craggy cliffs, and by treacherous salt marshes on a third, Alvar knew his fortified manor house to be virtually impenetrable. The men who had followed him to fight for Henry Tudor's cause were loyal to their own lord first and the King second. They would defend Alvar Manor against all comers.

So it was not fear that stayed his hand, but the oath of fealty he had sworn which was sacred to him. These past few days he had come close to breaking that vow a dozen times, yet he held back despite the hot desire which churned in him at the sight of Elspeth. Had Nessie but known it, her kinswoman was protected by a stronger hand than hers. For the journey at least Elspeth was safe.

As they neared their journey's end, Elspeth began to wonder what awaited her in London. Several times she played with the idea of asking Alvar what was to become of her, but pride held her back. She would not let him guess that she was afraid! He treated her with a cold disdain which showed how much he despised her. He was cruel and hateful and she detested him! Yet at times she was drawn to him against her will.

Riding just behind him day after day, her eyes dwelt often on his proud, straight back, noticing the way his black hair curled softly on his collar. She could not fail to be aware of how his men responded instantly to his every command, but somehow she did not think it was fear which held them loyal to him.

Once she asked the man he had appointed her bodyguard for the day why he served Alvar.

The man stared at her as though she was mad, then: 'I serve him because he is Alvar,' he said.

There was a note of pride in his voice as he spoke and Elspeth was puzzled. Could he be proud to serve a man who murdered in cold blood? Surely such men did not inspire devotion but only fear! Yet Alvar had murdered

Baron Cassell in order to steal his new wife, that much was certain.

Alvar filled her thoughts more than she cared for. She was afraid of him—and yet she no longer believed that he would carry out his threat against her brothers. Why had he said such a terrible thing—had it been to protect her from herself? Elspeth knew that if he had not made the threat she might have tried to take her own life. He had made the one threat which would force her to go on living despite her grief and her fears. She was his prisoner more surely than if he had bound her with chains.

'He is evil and wicked,' she told herself. 'He serves my father's enemy, and I would be revenged on him if I could. And yet . . .'

And yet when Firkin had planned to kill him she had been seized with a feeling of terror that was not all concern for her brothers. There were times he looked at her when she had the oddest sensation. She caught herself staring at his strong, sensual mouth and wondering what it would be like to be kissed by him. The next moment she was covered in confusion and shame. What was she thinking of?

Alvar was hateful and cruel. Better she should die than be kissed by him!

CHAPTER FOUR

WHEN Henry Tudor first reached London after his triumph on the field of Bosworth, the city threw itself into a paroxysm of rejoicing, indulging in a flood of feasts, miracle plays and countless other frivolities. But by the end of September, when Alvar's party reached the city, London was in the grip of a contagious fever known as the sweating sickness.

The King moved to Kennington, and it was there that Elspeth was first brought into his presence. She sank into a deep curtsey before him, raising her eyes nervously to his as he told her to rise; and found herself gazing into a pair of keen blue eyes. Henry Tudor was well-built, a little above average height with a strong rather than handsome face. His hair was short and he wore a flat, black velvet hat. Elspeth thought he had more the look of a scholar than a soldier, and she discovered that she found him less terrifying than Alvar.

'Lady Elspeth, you are welcome at our court if you come in friendship,' he said, his thin lips risking a faint smile. 'You are my ward and I shall find you a position in the Princess Elizabeth's household—if you will first swear an oath of allegiance to me.'

Elspeth stared at him in surprise. 'Then . . . I am not to be a prisoner in the Tower?'

Henry's shrewd eyes glinted with amusement as he turned to Alvar. 'It would be a crime to shut such beauty away from the world, would it not, Alvar? Methinks you have proved too stern a warden.' But when he looked again at Elspeth the smile had gone. 'Well, lady, will you swear loyalty to your king and let the past be forgotten?'

Elspeth hesitated. The wound dealt her by her father's death was still raw—but he had died honourably on the field of battle. His cause was lost and surely there was no shame in admitting defeat when there was no other course open to her?

'For myself I would gladly do as you ask, Sire—but what of my brothers? Are they to be offered the same choice?'

'Your brothers have already sworn fealty to me, Lady Elspeth. I have placed them in households loyal to me, there they will be safe from temptation—and perhaps in time may take their appointed place at court.'

'And what of my father's lands?' Elspeth shivered with fear as she saw his quick frown, knowing that she pushed him too far.

'Your father chose to take up arms against me,' Henry said, and his voice was suddenly harsh. 'His lands are forfeit—once Parliament is joined all those who committed treason against their rightful king will find themselves the poorer. Be grateful I offer you your freedom and do not try my patience further!'

It was on the tip of Elspeth's tongue to retort that Henry Tudor was merely a pretender to the throne when her father rode against him, and therefore the Earl of Murran had committed no treason; but a warning look from Alvar silenced her. It was useless to argue unless she wished to find herself a prisoner in the Tower after all. Henry Tudor was now the undoubted King of England, and she must be grateful he had seen fit to offer her freedom and a place in the household of his future queen. After all, Elspeth was only a woman. Her father was dead, her brothers virtual prisoners—what else could she do but accept the King's decision?

She curtsied to him once more, lowering her long lashes to veil the anger she felt inside. 'I thank Your Majesty for your most generous offer and do swear ever to be a loyal and loving subject.'

Henry smiled. 'Good. You shall rest here tonight,

lady, and tomorrow you shall be conveyed to the house of Elizabeth Woodville. There you shall remain until such time as I decide to take the Princess Elizabeth as my wife.'

Elspeth thanked him. The audience was at an end and she curtsied to him as she left the room.

Alvar bowed to the King. 'I ask your permission to escort the Lady Elspeth to her chamber, Sire.'

Henry's eyes flickered over him consideringly. 'As you wish, Alvar—but return immediately. I wish to speak with you on other matters.'

Alvar bowed once more and joined Elspeth.

Elspeth was silent as he accompanied her through the cold, echoing passages. She was comforted by the sight of his familiar figure, knowing that she would have been lost in the maze of endless rooms and too shy to enquire her way. Yet she did not want to admit that she felt grateful to him. Outside the room which was to be hers, Alvar halted, his eyes thoughtful as they travelled over her face.

'You will find your kinswoman inside, lady.'

Elspeth regarded him doubtfully. 'I cannot thank you, sir, for I am not grateful to have been brought here as your prisoner—and yet I would not have us part as bitter enemies.'

'What then—would you have me as a friend?' Alvar's eyes glowed suddenly with a clear blue flame. 'Oh no, lady, I do not think we could ever be friends—lovers perhaps. Yes, I think that might just be possible.' His fingers curled around her waist, making her wince as he held her tighter than he knew. 'Will you come with me to Alvar, Elspeth? Will you come of your own free will?'

Elspeth felt her heart leap in her breast. Her chest felt so tight that she could scarcely breathe. 'W-what are you saying?' she stammered, a shiver of something akin to fear running through her. 'Are you asking me to be your wife?'

Alvar smiled then; a cold, cruel smile which made her

shrink away from him. In an instant he had changed to a bitter stranger, something in his eyes making her gasp in dismay. 'No, lady, I was not asking you to marry me. What have you to offer me? You are the daughter of a traitor. You have no home, no fortune—why should I wed you? I admit you have some charms, and I would not be averse to finding you in my bed . . .'

Elspeth's hand snaked out, and this time he was not quick enough to stop her. She left a bloody trail across his cheek where her nails caught the skin.

Alvar looked startled. 'You little she-wolf!' he snarled. 'Sink your claws into me, would you? I'll teach you to think twice before you make the same mistake again!'

Elspeth stared at him in horror, too shocked by her own action to move away from him. He seized her roughly, pulling her close to him and tipping her head back, one hand circling her slender throat. For a moment Elspeth thought he was going to break her neck, then his mouth came down to crush hers into aching submission. Only then did she begin to struggle, but he held her fast, exploring her mouth with his tongue, sucking her sweetness as though he would devour her.

Elspeth fought furiously against the tumultuous clamouring his kiss aroused in her blood. Gradually she felt herself weakening as his mouth held hers prisoner, refusing to let her go. A wild joy was sweeping through her, making her want to respond fiercely to his demands. Her mind told her that she hated him; but her body betrayed her. She was hardly aware of what she did as her arms went up around his neck, her fingers sliding into his soft hair. She arched against him, knowing herself lost as his lips slid down her throat, searing her with a white-hot flame.

Abruptly, Alvar let her go. She staggered back, almost falling, her cheeks burning with shame as she saw the mockery in his eyes.

Elspeth pressed the back of her hand against her

mouth, rubbing as if she would scrub off the taste of his lips. 'You vile brute,' she whispered. 'I think I hate you. Do you hear me? I hate you!'

Alvar laughed softly. 'Love me or hate me, Elspeth, it is all one to me. But be sure of this—one day I shall make you beg me to love you. I promise you that!'

Elspeth covered her face with her hands as the shame washed over her. How could she have been so lost to all modesty as to let Alvar kiss her that way? It was bad enough that he had forced himself on her—but she had responded to his passion like a bitch in heat! He knew that she had surrendered to him utterly. He knew it and he was gloating over his triumph! At that moment Elspeth vowed that she would never let him break down her resistance like that again. She would rather die!

'Go away,' she hissed. 'I will never, never be your mistress!'

Alvar's smile mocked her. 'Protest as much as you like, lady. Your words deny me—but your body speaks truly. At the moment you are safe from me, but take care not to offend the King—for once you lose his protection you are mine.'

Elspeth wrenched at the latch of the door to her room, hearing his chilling laughter as she closed it hurriedly behind her. She leaned against it, trembling.

Nessie ceased unfolding a fresh gown to look at her. 'What troubles you, dearest?' she asked, seeing the girl's white face. 'Never say the King has condemned you to the Tower?'

'No. I am to serve the Princess Elizabeth,' Elspeth whispered, her throat dry.

'Then—what ails you?'

'Alvar—he frightens me.'

Nessie looked puzzled. 'But surely you are safe enough now? If Alvar meant to harm you, he would have taken advantage of you on our journey here.'

Elspeth shook her head, her eyes wild. 'You do not understand! Oh, Nessie, I am so afraid . . .'

Nessie put her arms around the trembling girl. 'That wicked, evil man!' she said fiercely. 'Do not fret, Elspeth, I will kill him myself before I let him harm you!'

At this, Elspeth released herself from Nessie's arms, a faint smile flickering for a moment about her mouth. 'Forget my foolishness, Nessie. Alvar cannot touch me as long as I remain the King's ward.' She laughed suddenly. 'I was more fortunate than I knew when Henry Tudor decided to keep me under his eyes. Besides, tomorrow we leave here for the Queen-Dowager's house—then I shall see no more of Alvar!'

Elspeth dressed hastily. Today, 16th January 1486, was an important day. At last Elizabeth of York, Princess of England, was to wed Henry Tudor. Though Henry had been crowned with great pomp and splendour in the October of 1485, he had shown no real desire to keep his promise to marry the Princess. Indeed, there were many amongst the Yorkist party who considered that he had slighted his future queen, not the least of these was the Queen-Dowager herself, Elizabeth Woodville.

Her own toilette complete, Elspeth hurried along the lofty passages to the Princess Elizabeth's apartments. She was amongst the fortunate ladies selected to help her mistress prepare for her wedding, and to accompany the Princess on her procession to the abbey. And afterwards Elspeth would be present at the banquet in the Palace of Westminster.

When Elspeth first came to Elizabeth Woodville's house she had been nervous of her new position in life. She had lived quietly in her father's castle, and she had been afraid she would not please her new mistress. However, the Princess was a good-natured girl of some twenty years, with the flaxen hair of the Plantagenets and a serene, pretty face. She had welcomed Elspeth warmly, bringing the girl close to tears when she expressed her sorrow at the Earl of Murran's death.

The Queen-Dowager, who seemed to Elspeth to exert

great influence over her daughter, had gone even further. In the privacy of her chamber she told Elspeth that she considered the Earl a brave man who had been martyred in a worthy cause—strange words from the mother of Henry Tudor's future queen.

But Elspeth knew there was little love lost between the King and Elizabeth Woodville. Henry had never forgiven her for scheming to have her daughter marry Richard III, and so hamper Henry's own bid for the throne. That she had done so was certain fact, even though such a marriage between uncle and niece would have been an incestuous one. What was not certain was whether the Princess had agreed to the match. She herself denied it strongly, despite all the rumours. Elspeth was inclined to believe her innocent of any plotting, and merely the tool of her ambitious mother.

However, the politics of the court were far from Elspeth's mind as she joined the other ladies in the Princess's apartments. She was excited by the prospect of seeing her mistress wed to the King, as were the other ladies; but uppermost in her mind was a conversation she had had with her Aunt Ursula the previous day.

Hearing of Elspeth's arrival in London, Aunt Ursula had lost no time in contacting her niece. She had once been a lady-in-waiting to the Queen-Dowager, and she was delighted that Elspeth was installed in her house. She had been allowed to visit Elspeth, and to send an escort so that Elspeth might visit her occasionally.

Lady Ursula was a strong-minded woman who had survived two marriages arranged for her by her father and then her brother. She had cared for neither of her husbands, but she had done her duty without complaint, giving birth to three sons, all of whom died in their infancy. Now in her middle years, wealthy and childless, Ursula had decided to take Elspeth under her wing. Ursula had always done her duty, and she considered it her duty to see Elspeth safely married. And last night she had confided her plans to Elspeth as they sat before the fire, saying suddenly:

'Elspeth, we must speak of your marriage.'

Elspeth had been so surprised that she could only stare at her aunt. 'My marriage?' she repeated foolishly.

Ursula frowned, her brows snapping together. 'Do you not wish to be married? Have you no desire for a home of your own—and children?'

'I had not thought of it,' Elspeth replied, not quite honestly. She had wondered if she would ever be free to marry, but her thoughts were confused and she did not want to confess them to her aunt.

'Then think of it now, girl,' her aunt said snappishly. 'Your position at court is not an easy one. The King could change his mind and send you to exile in some isolated fortress at any time. He might even decide you would be better locked away in a nunnery. But perhaps you would prefer that to marriage?'

'No!' Elspeth's shock registered in her face. 'Oh, aunt, you do not think he would do that—do you?'

Ursula gave a little secret smile. 'Kings are capricious creatures, my dear—who knows what they will do?'

Elspeth frowned. It was a woman's duty to marry and bear her husband's sons, she had always known that. She had hoped that when the time came for her to wed she would fall in love with a man who would love her in return. Nanette had been lucky, though Elspeth had not thought so at first. She knew her aunt was not speaking of a love match; a marriage would be arranged with a man of suitable birth, and Elspeth would be expected to do her duty. It would be the end of all her dreams—but had she ever really believed in those foolish dreams?

Elspeth sighed. 'I will be guided by you, aunt—but could I not just stay as I am? The Princess is kind to me, and perhaps the King will not send me away.'

Ursula laughed. 'You would not need to leave the Princess Elizabeth's household—until you bear your husband's children, that is. It would simply make you more secure. Married to the right man you will be safe enough.'

'But who would wish to marry me? I have no fortune,' Elspeth said, her cheeks burning as she remembered Alvar's cruel taunts. 'And would His Majesty grant me permission to wed?'

Ursula folded her hands primly in her lap. 'You may leave the details to me, Elspeth. In the absence of my brother I consider myself your guardian. I shall do what I can for you, of that you may be sure.'

She had refused to say more, summoning her servants to escort Elspeth back to her room in the Queen-Dowager's house.

Elspeth slept little that night, tossing and turning on her bed as she sought to find a solution to her tangled emotions. She longed to be able to talk to someone who would understand, but she knew there was no hope of her being allowed to visit her sister. The trouble was that she did not know what she wanted from life. Did the future hold nothing more for her than submission to a husband she did not love?

'You are very quiet this morning, Lady Elspeth. I hope you are not ill?'

Elspeth jumped guiltily as Princess Elizabeth's voice broke into her thoughts. 'I beg your pardon, Highness. I was not attending.'

'I asked if you were ill—you look a trifle pale.'

Elspeth shook her head, forcing herself to forget her own problems. 'I slept badly last night. I think it must be excitement at your wedding, Highness.'

The Princess nodded, a flicker of something like fear passing across her normally placid face. 'I too slept little last night,' she said. 'I have looked forward to this day so long—and yet now it is here I am afraid. I am afraid His Majesty will not find me pleasing.'

'What nonsense is this?' snapped the Queen-Dowager, frowning. 'Henry Tudor cannot fail to be pleased with you—you are the daughter of a king!'

'Yes, mama.' The Princess sighed. 'But I would be happier if we could at least like each other.'

'You foolish girl! At last you are to take your rightful place as Queen of England. You must put all this nonsense from your head and do your duty.'

'Yes, mama.' The Princess looked at her face in the small hand-mirror Elspeth brought her. 'I am ready.'

Elspeth smiled as she took back the mirror. 'You look beautiful,' she whispered. 'The King cannot fail to love you.'

The Princess smiled a little sadly. 'Thank you, Lady Elspeth. I pray that you are right.'

Following her mistress down to the crowd of waiting courtiers and the carriages which were to carry them to the great abbey, Elspeth realised how brave the Princess was. She well knew that Henry Tudor was marrying her only to make his throne more secure. The most she could hope for was that she might like her husband, any happiness she found in the future was most likely to come from her children. Yet she had accepted her fate without complaint.

Elspeth sighed, abandoning the struggle within herself. She too would do her duty when the time came. Like the Princess Elizabeth, she had no choice.

The Princess was greeted with enthusiastic, cheering crowds as she rode to her wedding, and when she returned with her husband to the banquet in Westminster Hall. If King Henry VII was displeased that the people lining the streets cheered louder for his wife than for himself, he gave no outward sign of it that day. He treated her with a polite deference which delighted the people. At last it seemed that England's troubles were over now that the Red and White Roses were joined as one.

The great hall at Westminster had been hung with cloth of gold, and the banners of both Lancaster and York hung from the huge wooden spans vaulting the roof. Fresh rushes and aromatic herbs had been strewn on the stone floors; and trestle tables had been set up in two long lines on either side of the room. The high table, where the King would sit with his new wife and his most important nobles, was set on a raised dais at the far end, beneath a canopy of golden cloth.

After attending to the Princess, Elspeth went to take her own place at one of the tables. She was not important enough to sit near the high table; for although she was the daughter of an Earl, her new status was that of a well-born servant. Most of the ladies and gentlemen seated at the tables took their turn to serve either the King or one of the leading nobles, for such was the fashion of the day. They themselves were waited on by the lesser gentry, who would eat their own meal in a smaller hall served by yeomen servants.

Walking to her seat at the lower end of the hall, Elspeth gave a cry of delight as she saw that she was placed one seat away from someone she had longed to see. She craned her neck to catch Nanette's eye, leaning out behind the young man between them to call her sister's name.

Lady Nanette's face lit up with pleasure. 'Elspeth—my dearest!' she cried. 'I had no idea you would be here today. Harold—look who is here!'

The young man sitting between them smiled at Elspeth, offering to exchange places with her, though it meant he moved further down the table to a place of lesser degree.

Elspeth accepted eagerly, giving him a warm smile, liking his gentle manners and pleasant face. 'How kind you are,' she said. 'I have not seen my sister for more than two years.'

He made her an elegant bow. 'Then I am delighted to be of service to you. May I know your name?'

'Yes. Yes, of course.' Elspeth blushed, made shy by the evident admiration in his eyes. 'I am Elspeth Murran—daughter of the late Earl of Murran.'

'I am honoured to make your acquaintance, Lady Elspeth,' he said, a flicker of new interest in his liquid brown eyes. 'I am Philip Rathbone. A sometime poet and the younger son of an undistinguished country squire of whom you will know nothing. I, on the other hand, know much of your father. He was a brave man.'

'Thank you,' Elspeth said, veiling her eyes with her long lashes. 'But for your own sake, sir, you should guard your tongue. My father has been condemned as a traitor.'

Philip Rathbone's eyes kindled with an angry flame. 'He is not alone, lady—many others have been served in a similar way.' Suddenly he laughed self-consciously. 'But I detain you—and you must be anxious to speak with your sister.'

He turned away and Elspeth sat down beside Nanette. 'Oh, my dearest sister,' she whispered, her voice choking with emotion as her hand crept beneath the table to clasp Nanette's. 'It is so long since I saw you! I hoped you might be here today. Aunt Ursula said that Sir Harold had been ill . . . ?'

Nanette gave her husband an anxious glance. 'It is true. Harold has not been well of late. But we were summoned to attend His Majesty's wedding to the Princess and we dare not risk offending the King.'

Elspeth nodded. 'I understand. Your husband took no part in the fighting so you have not been stripped of your lands; but it is known that Sir Harold was once Richard's servant.'

Nanette frowned. 'Hush, my love, do not speak of it. We go in fear of our lives as it is. After all, I am the Earl of Murran's eldest daughter.'

Elspeth's fingers closed tightly around her sister's hand. 'We live in dangerous times, Nan, we must all take care.'

'Yes.' Nanette's eyes were serious as she studied her sister's lovely face. 'And what of you, Elspeth, are you well?'

Elspeth shrugged. 'Well enough—better for seeing you. Oh, Nan, I do wish we could be together. If only our father had allowed me to come to you before all this happened!'

Nanette's smile was tinged with sadness. 'It seems we are fated to be separated, my dearest. First by our father—and now by the King. He would never allow you to make your home with us. He would think we were at the root of some plot against him.'

Elspeth sighed. 'I know.' Her pretty face darkened with rebellion. 'We are as much prisoners as if he had shut us in the Tower!'

Nanette shook her head. 'No, my love, you must not give way to despair. Harold and I come to London occasionally. We may be able to meet at Aunt Ursula's house sometimes.'

The storm clouds faded from Elspeth's eyes. 'Then I suppose I must be satisfied. At least, I will save my anger for when we part. We have tonight, and I am so happy I could shout with joy.'

Nanette laughed. 'You impetuous child,' she said lovingly. 'I see you have not changed.'

'Nor have you.' Elspeth smiled. 'Well, have you any news for me? When I had your last letter—ages ago!—you thought you might be with child. Am I an aunt?'

Nanette sighed. 'Alas no, it was but a false alarm. But I do not give up hope. Perhaps God will grant us the boon of a child one day. If not . . .' She shrugged her shoulders. 'Harold is a good man: I am content.'

Elspeth squeezed her hand. 'I know. I am glad you married him. I want you always to be happy.'

Nanette smiled tenderly. 'If I could see you settled with a man as kind as my husband—then I should indeed be happy. I suppose there is no one you want to marry?'

Elspeth gave her head a little shake, averting her eyes. 'No—no one,' she said. 'Oh, do look, Nan, the tumblers are going to perform for us. See the dwarf with his bladder—what an ugly little creature he is!'

'I think he looks sad.'

Elspeth looked again. 'Yes, he does,' she said, pity stirring in her heart. 'The poor little man—see how the others taunt him.' She half rose in her seat as one of the tumblers seized the dwarf and threw him through the air. 'Oh! they will hurt him. It is too cruel.'

Philip Rathbone turned to smile at her. 'Do not worry, Lady Elspeth,' he said, a note of reassurance in his voice. 'He knows how to land. Watch—now he will take his revenge.'

Suddenly the little man bounded across the floor with a series of lightning somersaults, butting his assailant in the stomach with his hard head, which looked too big for his body. The assembled courtiers roared with laughter as the tall man doubled up with pain, and the little creature began to caper round him, tormenting him with the pig's bladder he carried on the end of a stick. It quickly became clear that the dwarf was more than a match for his opponent, his legs moving almost as rapidly as his wickedly sarcastic tongue.

The performance was soon over, and the tumblers prepared to leave the hall. But before they went the dwarf stopped, seeming to look all around the room; then he came bounding across the floor, ending up immediately in front of Elspeth. He bowed low, his eyes full of mischief.

'Lady,' he cried in his high voice. 'You are the fairest damsel I have ever seen. I vow you have stolen my heart away. I am dying of love for you—will you not let me kiss your hand? Even though I am an ugly little monster . . .'

Elspeth blushed as the courtiers roared with laughter, but then anger stirred in her. The dwarf was after all a man, though he must go through life imprisoned in his crooked body. She held out her hand to him with a smile.

'I would be honoured, sir,' she said, lifting her head a little higher as she felt all eyes turn upon her.

The crowd hushed as the little man bowed over her hand, waiting for the fun to begin, expecting her to repulse him at the last moment. She did not, nor did she draw away from him as he pressed his lips to her skin.

He looked up at her, his eyes very bright. 'God bless you,' he said quietly. 'I am always your servant—remember me for I shall remember you.'

All at once he darted forward and tapped Philip Rathbone on the shoulders with his pig's bladder. 'I dub you Knight of Misrule,' he said. 'Beware the serpent beneath the skin.' Then he bounded across the floor with a series of fast somersaults.

The courtiers laughed and clapped, relieved that he had hidden his true nature behind a clown's face again. Elspeth did not laugh, there was something terribly sad about the little man. She had seen it for a brief moment as she looked into his eyes.

The musicians had begun to play now, and the King gave his permission for the courtiers to dance if they wished. Several couples were already forming circles when Philip Rathbone turned to Elspeth.

'Will you honour me with this dance, Lady Elspeth?'

Elspeth's cheeks tinged with colour. 'I am not sure if I ought,' she said. 'We have not been formally introduced, sir.'

Nanette smiled at her. 'No one will know if you do not tell them, Elspeth—and Mr Rathbone was kind enough to give you his seat.'

Elspeth gave a little gurgle of laughter. 'Well, if you think it is proper, Nan. I shall be happy to dance with you, sir.'

'Good.' Philip smiled at her, giving her his hand and leading her out into the middle of the floor.

Elspeth found that they were well matched, for he was not above average height and she did not have to strain up to look at him. He was slim, his light brown hair a little longer than was fashionable and curled under sleekly. And despite his declaration that he was merely the younger son of a country squire, he wore a magnificent ruby ring on the little finger of his right hand.

He was also an excellent dancer, she discovered.

'You put me to shame, sir—where did you learn to dance so elegantly?'

She thought his eyes took on a guarded expression as he replied: 'Here—there—anywhere. I am a wandering minstrel. I come and go as I please.'

Elspeth looked at him curiously. 'Are you really a poet?'

He smiled. 'Some would say so—others are less kind. But you shall judge for yourself. I will write a sonnet just for you.'

'Will you really?' Elspeth gazed up at him in delight, unaware of the sparkling beauty of her own face.

'If you will allow me—it will be my pleasure.'

'Oh yes; please do,' Elspeth cried. 'I have never had a sonnet written just for me before.'

'Then all the men you have met must either be blind or soulless. Do you not know how beautiful you are?'

Elspeth flushed at the look in his smiling eyes. 'Oh no! You must not say so. Please do not flatter me, sir. I would rather we dealt honestly with each other.'

'I swear on my honour as a gentleman—you are the most beautiful woman I have ever seen. God's body! That dwarf was right. You put every other woman here to shame.'

Elspeth veiled her eyes. 'I think we should return to my sister now.'

'I have not offended you, sweet lady?'

Elspeth shook her head. 'No, I am not offended, sir.'

'Then I may still write my sonnet for you?'

'Yes,' Elspeth murmured shyly. 'If you wish.'

'I do.' Philip bowed over her hand. 'I will take you back to your sister now.'

Elspeth dared not look at him as they returned to their places. She was not quite sure how to handle his extravagant compliments. Philip Rathbone had the practised tongue and the exquisite manners of a man used to moving in circles other than those of a country gentleman, of that she was sure.

She drank a little of her wine, watching the dancers form new sets for the next dance. Lost in her own reflections, she was not aware of the man striding purposefully towards her until his voice scattered her thoughts, startling her and causing the colour to drain from her face.

'Lady Elspeth,' Alvar made her a mocking bow. 'May I claim the privilege of kinship and hope that you will honour me with this dance?'

Elspeth glanced up at him, fighting against the wild racing of her heart. She wished she might refuse him, but knew that she dare not deny his request having shown herself willing to dance with Mr Rathbone. She stood up and laid her arm lightly on his, struggling to conceal her nervousness.

'As you wish, my lord.'

'So formal?' His eyes glinted dangerously. 'You looked more kindly on your last partner, I think.'

Elspeth's head shot up, glaring at him. 'I have little reason to smile at you, sir. I have not forgotten our last meeting!'

He laughed softly, his fingers closing possessively about her wrist. 'As if I could forget,' he murmured. 'Do not think yourself free of me because we have not met since that day. I have been away on business for His Majesty—but I am back now.'

Elspeth trembled as his arm encircled her waist. She would have given anything to run from him, but she knew she dare not. She must suffer his nearness for the duration of the dance, and she must appear calm and unconcerned. She found it almost unbearable, the touch of his hands sending little shivers of fear through her at every step. But at last the music ended and Alvar conducted her back to her seat at Nanette's side.

'I shall see you anon, Lady Elspeth,' he said, his manner deceptively charming now. 'Lady Nanette, I trust you and my cousin are both well?'

Nanette gave him her gentle smile. 'Yes, I thank you, Lord Alvar. When may we hope to see you in our house? Harold often speaks of you—you are always welcome.'

Alvar's face softened. His voice was almost seductively caressing as he replied: 'I do know that, madam. The King's affairs bind me to him for the present—but I will visit you one day. Will you forgive me if I take Sir Harold away from you for a while?'

'Of course,' Nanette smiled at him again as he paused to whisper something to her husband.

'I shall not be long, my dear,' Sir Harold said. 'You have Elspeth to keep you company.'

Elspeth watched as they walked away together, a little shiver running through her. 'I hope Sir Harold will come to no harm—I do not trust Alvar.'

Nanette looked surprised. 'Alvar would not harm his own cousin—why should you think he might?'

Elspeth shrugged. Alvar was Nanette's cousin by marriage, she could not tell her that he was an evil man. Nanette would not believe her—unless she told her the whole story. And Elspeth was much too ashamed to do that!

'Oh—I was just thinking of what Nessie told us about him when he came to stay for your wedding.'

Nanette nodded. 'I know and it was true—except that Nessie did not know everything.' She hesitated, frowning. 'I would like to tell you the truth, Elspeth, but Harold made me promise never to tell anyone. But do not think too harshly of Alvar—he is not as wicked as you believe.'

Elspeth digested her sister's words in silence. Nanette always tried to think well of everyone, naturally she would find excuses for her husband's cousin if she could. She simply did not know Alvar as thoroughly as Elspeth did. She had not been humiliated by him!

Elspeth sipped her wine. 'I suppose not—but I cannot like him.'

Nanette sighed. 'Well, you cannot help that—but do

try not to offend him, my dear. After all, he does have the King's ear . . .'

Elspeth shivered, she knew that only too well. She had recovered her composure these past months, believing Alvar had decided to let her be since he made no attempt to visit her at Elizabeth Woodville's house. Now she felt she was walking a narrow precipice: one false step and she would plunge into the chasm below!

Alvar was always there, lurking in the shadows like the wolf he was named, waiting for her to fall.

CHAPTER FIVE

FOR several weeks after that night, Elspeth found herself tortured by terrifying dreams which made her wake with a start, shivering and with a foolish desire to weep. She did her best to hide her nightmares from Nessie, but it was not easy as her kinswoman slept in a small alcove leading off Elspeth's chamber. More often than not she would come to see what had made the girl cry out in her sleep.

Apart from the dreams Elspeth found the life at the palace pleasant enough. Her duties were not arduous, and she was often allowed a few free hours to visit her aunt. Ursula had not mentioned marriage again, except to say that she had formed her plans. Elspeth was content to leave it at that for the present.

If she had been a vain girl, she might have had her head turned by all the attention she had begun to attract from the courtiers. At the Queen-Dowager's house they had lived quietly, not receiving many gentlemen callers, and so her beauty had passed unnoticed. But all that had changed since the banquet at Westminster. The sad dwarf had not been the only one who thought Elspeth the loveliest woman at court. And, as the celebrations continued day after day, Elspeth found herself surrounded by eager gallants, all wanting to share her leisure moments.

Whenever there was dancing she was besieged with partners, and she could not walk in the palace gardens without collecting a bevy of followers. Already, three of her admirers had declared themselves in love with her, and several gentlemen had composed sonnets to her beauty.

The first to present her with a set of verses was Philip Rathbone. He had decided to praise her lovely eyes, calling them dark pools of mystery, and vowing she was an enchantress who wove invisible threads around men's hearts to ensnare them.

Elspeth was delighted with his poem, especially as he sang it to her in his deep, melodious voice while he sat at her feet in the gardens, sending her long, languishing looks. He had not yet declared himself in love with her, but he was one of her most devoted admirers, and Elspeth found him the most pleasing of her new companions. For though the other gentlemen made her laugh with their outrageous compliments, she did not believe them when they spoke of love. She thought many of them rather shallow creatures, loving only their fine peacock clothes. She was happiest when Philip played his viol for her or sang a few verses of one of his songs.

'Why do you look so sad, Lady Elspeth?' he asked one day when they had managed to move a little apart from the other courtiers in the great hall. 'Have you some secret sorrow in your heart? Will you not tell me? You must know I am your friend . . .'

Elspeth smiled slightly, touching his hand. 'Yes, I do believe you my friend, sir—but there is nothing you can do to help me.'

'Are you sure?' His voice dropped to a whisper. 'I would do anything to serve you.'

Elspeth's cheeks burned as she saw the ardent look in his eyes. 'You are very kind and I am grateful for your concern—but if I am sad it is because I miss my sister.'

'You are still grieving for your father—is that not so?'

'Yes—a little.' Elspeth sighed. 'Death brings so many regrets. But it is my sister I miss the most. I wish—oh, how I wish I was free to choose my own life!'

'If the Tudor tyrant were dead and the true king on the throne of England you would not need to sigh so, my lady.'

Elspeth turned pale, glancing anxiously over her

shoulder lest anyone was close enough to hear. 'Be careful, sir! If His Majesty were to learn of this you would pay for it with your life.'

Philip smiled, unconcerned. 'But you would not betray me, Lady Eslpeth—you are the Earl of Murran's daughter.'

'Yes, and because of it I am the King's ward and must stay where he can watch me.'

Philip took her hand and kissed it. 'It gives me pain to see you so unhappy, lady—but do not despair. The time may yet come when you will be free to follow your heart again.'

'Hush,' Elspeth whispered. 'Say no more—Alvar is watching us. I think he is coming this way . . .'

Philip picked up his viol, running his fingers over it lightly as Lord Alvar walked purposefully towards them.

'Lady Elspeth, where have all your gallants gone? I trust they do not begin to desert you?' His blue eyes flickered coldly over Philip. 'I have been trying to remember where I have seen you before, sir. I think it may have been in Flanders.'

Philip continued to strum his viol, shrugging his shoulders. 'Who knows, my lord? My travels take me to many lands—but I do not recall your face.'

Elspeth gasped as she heard the insult implied in Philip's words. The two men were glaring at each other with barely-concealed hatred in their eyes. For some reason they had taken an instant dislike to one another. She looked at them anxiously; Alvar, cold and proud in his usual black; and Philip, slighter and fairer, dressed in the gay blue and silver he favoured. The mere sight of Alvar was enough to send most men scurrying away with a muttered excuse, but Philip Rathbone did not seem to fear him. Indeed, his smile was derisive, as though inviting a challenge from Alvar.

Feeling the tension grow between them, Elspeth was driven to desperate measures. Turning to Alvar, she smiled up at him. 'Will you give me your arm, my lord? I was about to return to Her Majesty's apartments—and I wanted to ask a favour of you.'

Alvar looked surprised, as well he might since Elspeth normally went out of her way to avoid him. He was not one of the gallants who dangled after her. In fact they had spoken no more than a few words in passing since they danced at Westminster, though they were both very much aware of each other whenever they chanced to meet.

'I should be honoured,' he replied, a hint of mockery in his voice as he offered her his arm.

Elspeth laid her hand lightly upon his, trying to control the shiver which ran through her. She gave Philip a faint smile as they moved away. Leaving the throng of courtiers gathered in the vast hall, they began to walk up a wide flight of stairs and along a gallery hung with magnificent tapestries.

Alvar glanced at her pale face, guessing something of what was in her mind. 'This is indeed an honour, Lady Elspeth,' he said, his voice toneless, though his eyes gleamed for a moment with something which might have been amusement. 'You arouse my curiosity. I cannot but wonder what is of such importance that you deliberately seek my company.'

Elspeth flushed. She had acted on the spur of the moment, thinking only to prevent a clash between the two men. Desperately, she sought for an excuse and found one.

'I had a letter from Nanette yesterday,' she said. 'Harold has been ill again and she is worried . . .' Suddenly Elspeth looked up at him, no longer making an excuse but speaking from her heart. 'Nanette and I were always so close before she married. I want so much to be with her now she needs me. If only I could be there to comfort her . . .'

Alvar frowned. 'And what do you want of me, lady?'

Elspeth's hand trembled on his arm. 'If anyone could persuade the King to listen to my plea it is you. Could you not ask him to allow me this favour? It would only be for a short time—and I would take an oath that I will not seek to plot against His Majesty!'

Alvar looked at her oddly. 'Does this visit mean so very much to you? Are you terribly unhappy here at court?'

Elspeth could not bear to meet his eyes. 'Yes,' she whispered, a single tear escaping to trickle down her cheek. 'Please, my lord, for pity's sake, help me.'

She raised her head then, her eyes full of a desperate appeal which reminded him of a fawn he had once found in the forest after a hunting party had killed its mother. For the first time in many years something stirred in the heart Alvar believed long dead. He recognised the emotion and crushed it ruthlessly before it became too strong and destroyed him. He had once known how to love, but that was before he had stood on the very brink of hell and gazed down into the fiery pit. Never again would he let himself be swayed by a woman's tears—no matter how lovely she was!

His face hardened. 'I fear I can do nothing for you, Lady Elspeth. Such a request would only serve to bring down Henry's wrath on your head—and mine. He will not hold you for ever. You must be patient and wait until the time is right. Now, if you will excuse me, I have business I must attend to.'

Elspeth watched as he strode away in the opposite direction. She felt close to tears. For a moment just now he had seemed as though he would help her. She had forgotten to be afraid as she looked up into his eyes, a feeling passing between them which was stronger than fear.

Elspeth dashed away her tears, telling herself she was being foolish. Her fate could have been so much worse. The Queen was kind to her. Her duties were not hard, and she had the freedom of the court—why must she seek so desperately to leave the palace? Why was she so very unhappy?

The answer came suddenly, like a flash of blinding light. She gasped, shaking her head as she tried to deny it. 'Oh no,' she whispered, the pain sliding into her heart like the blade of a sword. As a child she had given her love to a father who despised her for being a girl and not the son he wanted. Surely she could not be so foolish as to love again without hope of being loved in return!

Yet perhaps it was not surprising that she should love Alvar, despite the way he had treated her. He and her father were not unalike, and perhaps in her grief she had unconsciously substituted one for the other. The lonely heart did not always choose wisely; and when he had forced her to submit to his kiss, she had surrendered more than she realised. At least now she understood the wild dreams which disturbed her rest, and why they brought her to the brink of tears. For in her dreams Alvar became the tender lover she had always hoped to find. Unfortunately, her dreams were far from reality. Alvar might desire her as his mistress, but he would never love her. She did not think he was capable of loving.

Elspeth knew she must never let him guess her true feelings towards him. If he once learnt that she loved him, he would use her love as a weapon against her. He would force her to submit to him totally; and submission without love could bring her only pain. No, he must never, never know what was in her heart! She must let him believe she still hated him—or she was lost!

Elspeth's life was made easier by the King's decision to set out on a journey through his kingdom. Since Alvar was to accompany him, and Elspeth remained with the Queen and her court, she was saved the daily contact with him which caused her so much pain.

From time to time news reached them of the King's progress. He had reached Lincoln by early April, and it was there he learned of a planned uprising against him. Lord Lovell, formerly Richard III's chamberlain, together with the Staffords had left the sanctuary at

Colchester whence they had flown after the defeat at Bosworth. Their intentions were not at first known, and Henry proceeded towards York.

At Nottingham he discovered that Lord Lovell was marching on York with a force of 4,000 men, and that the Staffords were attacking Worcester with another army. After sending his uncle, Jasper Tudor, now the Duke of Bedford, in pursuit with an army of 3,000 fighting men, Henry left Nottingham. At Pontefract he was told that Lovell was preparing to fall on him as he entered the City of York. But though his enemies were now all around him, Henry's courage and keen brain did not desert him. He sent his uncle on ahead to offer a free pardon to all who would desert Lovell. Once again his shrewdness was to win the day. Lovell's supporters deserted him in droves, and Lovell himself fled in panic, taking refuge in a friend's house until he could quit England for the safety of the Duchess of Burgundy's court in Flanders.

The Staffords were not so lucky. They took sanctuary at Colnham, a little village near Abingdon, but they were dragged from their refuge, the elder brother dying at Tyburn.

After routing the rebels, Henry proceeded to York where he was greeted with much adulation and servile acclaim. He stayed there for three weeks while the citizens fêted him, holding great pageants in his honour.

When the news reached the Queen's court there was much relief, except perhaps on the part of the Queen-Dowager. Relations between Elizabeth Woodville and Henry Tudor remained difficult, despite the fact that the Queen was now carrying her husband's child.

Elspeth could not help noticing that Philip Rathbone was angered by the news of the King's bloodless victory. He mumbled about the foolishness of ill-prepared plans and too much haste. She was almost sure he had known something might happen during the King's journey, and she knew he longed for Henry's downfall. These days he was often to be seen in the Queen-Dowager's company, and Elspeth noticed him leaving her apartments on several occasions.

He continued to be one of Elspeth's admirers, though he had still not committed himself in any way. Sometimes he seemed to be on the verge of declaring himself, but Elspeth gently forestalled him. She did not know how to answer him. She did not love him, but he was kind and gentle and she felt she might find contentment as his wife. She had long since ceased to hope for happiness, and marriage to someone like Philip was the only escape for her. Perhaps if she could leave the court she could push the memory of Alvar from her mind.

Elspeth was a little surprised that her aunt had not spoken of her marriage again, but she supposed that the King's absence had delayed her aunt's plans. She wondered whether she dare mention Philip to Ursula.

Had she but known it, Lady Ursula's plans had so far met with a blank refusal from the King.

'I have my own plans for the Lady Elspeth,' he said when Ursula begged an audience with him before he left the capital. 'I shall dispose of her hand in my own good time.'

Lady Ursula had refused to give up, but she found that the match she had been set on was suddenly abandoned by the gentleman in question. It seemed he was not willing to risk the King's anger even for so lovely a bride as Elspeth, and the dowry her aunt had promised him.

To complicate matters more, Ursula had contracted an inflammation of the lungs in March which forced her to keep to her bed. Her condition, which was at first thought to be a mere chill, continued to deteriorate. Having been prepared for the worst all her life, Lady Ursula put her affairs in order and sent for Elspeth.

When she was shown into her aunt's bedchamber Elspeth was shocked by the change in her. Lady Ursula had always been a stout, healthy woman with a high complexion. Now her cheeks were sunken and her skin had a yellow tinge.

'Oh, Aunt Ursula, why did you not let me know you were ill before?' Elspeth cried, feeling guilty because she had not visited her for some weeks. 'If only I had known I would have come sooner. Forgive me for neglecting you.'

Ursula shook her head. 'Do not blame yourself, child. I did not intend you to know.' She beckoned to Elspeth, patting the heavy silk covers. 'Come and sit beside me, Elspeth. The doctors assure me that there is no risk of infection, and I want to look at you.'

Elspeth did as she was told. The room was stuffy and airless, the windows shuttered and barred to keep out the evil humours of the night air. The only light came from the huge fire burning in the grate. She touched her aunt's hand, feeling the skin damp and heated beneath her fingers.

'Are you too hot, aunt? Shall I dampen down the fire?'

'No—leave it be,' said Ursula testily. 'I am supposed to sweat—it relieves the body of the poisons which cause the illness. I shall be better presently.

Elspeth was silent. She was afraid her aunt was sicker than she realised. Or perhaps Lady Ursula knew the truth and was trying to spare her.

Ursula patted her hand wearily. 'You should not be anxious, Elspeth. If it is my time to die—then I am ready. I have lived long enough—and seen two husbands into their graves! They both died fighting for the cause they believed in—as your father did.' She sighed. 'You remind me so much of him. You should have been a boy. He was proud of you, you know. He told me you had more spirit than either of Margaret's whelps.'

Elspeth felt her eyes sting with tears. 'Did he? I wish he had told me.'

'He was proud and stubborn.' Lady Ursula sighed again. 'We Murrans are all proud and stubborn—except

Nanette. She is like her mother, too soft for her own good.'

Elspeth frowned. 'Nanette is very dear to me, aunt.'

Ursula gave a snort. 'We won't quarrel over Nanette, child. I haven't time for quarrels. You are the only true Murran left, that's why I wanted to see you safely wed. I am afraid I've failed you, Elspeth. I have not been able to arrange a marriage for you—and now it is too late.'

'Oh, surely not!' Elspeth cried, her fingers unconsciously tightening about her aunt's hand. 'You will get better—you must!'

'Perhaps.' Ursula made a wry face. 'But I have provided for you either way. All I have will be yours when I am gone—and I employed the finest lawyers in England to make certain Henry Tudor cannot legally take it from you! I'm no traitor and neither are you. All his cunning won't help him get his greedy hands on my money. He cannot benefit, even if you die . . .' Ursula laughed, relishing the thought of Henry's chagrin, then she was overtaken by a fit of coughing.

Elspeth bent over her anxiously. 'Do not try to speak any more, aunt. Will you not let me get you a glass of water?'

Ursula shook her head. 'Do not fuss, girl. I shall do well enough.'

'Is there nothing I can do for you?'

'No—yes, you may kiss my cheek.'

Elspeth bent and pressed her lips to Ursula's feverish skin. 'You are burning up,' she said, a note of alarm in her voice. 'Pray let me bring the physician to you.'

'So that he can bleed me again?' Ursula snorted. 'Physicians—quacks the lot of them! No, child, just leave me to rest now. And do not fret over me. I dare say I shall be better soon—but I wanted to make you safe.'

Elspeth bent to kiss her aunt's cheek again. 'I thank you for your care of me, but I would rather see you well again.'

Ursula smiled and patted her hand gently, then she

closed her eyes. Elspeth slid from the bed carefully so as not to disturb her. For a few moments she stood looking down at her aunt, then she walked quietly to the door, closing it behind her.

The next day Elspeth was obliged to accompany the Queen and her court to Winchester, there to await the birth of the heir to England's throne.

It was a month later that she heard of her aunt's death. Lady Ursula had left instructions that her niece was not to be told of her death until the burial was over and the lawyers had her affairs well in hand.

A bent, greying gentleman made the journey from London to tell her the news. His face was wizened with age, and his fingers so gnarled with arthritis that he could scarcely hold a quill; but his brain was sharp and alert. He mumbled into his scraggy beard as he tried to explain the details of Lady Ursula's will to the bewildered girl.

'But what does it all mean?' Elspeth asked, lost in the twists and turns of the legal terms.

The lawyer sighed. 'It is a most complicated will, Lady Elspeth. Your aunt was determined her money should not fall into the wrong hands. However, in simple terms it amounts to this—you will receive an income from a trust until you marry, at which time the trust can be broken only by your written consent. If you do not marry the trust continues and goes to the church when you die. If the trust is broken during your lifetime without your consent, then the money is to be distributed to the poor of London.'

'I see—then not even the King could break the trust?'

'Indeed not.' The lawyer smiled. 'Your aunt was a clever woman, Lady Elspeth. Not even His Majesty would risk the anger of the common folk of London if it was discovered that he had appropriated money which should rightfully be theirs. And the church has never been known to let go any money left to it . . .'

Elspeth smiled. 'I doubt His Majesty would find it

worth the trouble to try. So Aunt Ursula has her revenge in death. I pray she may rest in peace—and I thank you for your kindness in coming to see me, sir. I hope you will continue to look after my affairs, for I have no head for such things.'

The lawyer looked at her oddly, wondering if she really understood how wealthy her aunt had been. She did not seem in the least interested in the money itself, taking more pleasure in her aunt's cleverness. He considered explaining the extent of her aunt's estate, but decided against it. The girl was young and obviously unused to handling money. It might be better for her if she did not know how rich she was.

He smiled at her kindly. 'You may leave everything to me, Lady Elspeth—until you have a husband to take care of your affairs, of course.'

Elspeth sighed. 'That may be a long time, sir. I am not sure His Majesty will ever allow me to marry—or that I wish to be married.'

The old man pursed his lips thoughtfully. He considered it very likely that the King would choose to give his ward in marriage very soon. Henry Tudor was a parsimonious man who disliked spending his own wealth—what better way to reward one of his followers than to bestow a rich bride on him? Especially when there was no way he could appropriate the girl's fortune for himself! Still it was best not to speak of such matters, for a careless word could be misconstrued as treason.

The lawyer departed, leaving Elspeth alone in the small chamber where they had met. The Queen had given her special permission to use the room, and she knew she would not be disturbed. She sat looking out of the window, watching the courtiers strolling in the sunny courtyard below. Until this moment she had not realised how much she had come to rely on her aunt. Lady Ursula had always seemed so strong and confident. While she lived, Elspeth had felt there might be some future for her. She had let herself believe that her aunt might prevail upon the King to let her marry, now that foolish dream had gone the way of all the others.

Elspeth sighed. She had the appearance of freedom, but she was as much Henry Tudor's prisoner as if she was in the Tower itself.

The King had not so far chosen to join his wife at Winchester, but he might do so at any time. And when he came, Alvar would come with him.

Elspeth had never felt quite so alone before. Suddenly she bent her head and wept.

CHAPTER SIX

ELSPETH paused in the gallery, peering through the latticed stonework of the balustrade at the crowd of richly-dressed courtiers filling the great hall below. The room was vast, with huge stone pillars supporting the heavily-carved, vaulted roof; and at one end smoke occasionally belched out from the big, open fireplace where a log from the trunk of a tree burnt merrily. The scene was one of noise and confusion, but above the laughter and excited voices she could still hear the bells of the cathedral as they rang out joyously.

Today the city of Winchester was celebrating the christening of a prince. For on the 30th September 1486 the Queen had been safely delivered of a healthy male child.

Elspeth was looking for the tall figure of Alvar, her emotions torn between dread and hope. It was several months since she had seen him now, for he remained constantly with the King; and on his return from the north, Henry had chosen to reside at a convenient distance from the Queen's court, in the New Forest, seldom visiting his wife. His behaviour had not pleased the Yorkist party, many of whom had found themselves barred from positions they had expected to hold at court. However, today His Majesty had attended the christening of his son, and everyone was to join in the celebrations.

Elspeth was a little late, because she was one of the fortunate ladies chosen to see the young prince settled in his cot, and she had remained with his nurses until he was asleep. The child enchanted Elspeth. He was a beautiful babe; and her new duties gave her a great deal of pleasure. Perhaps that was why she had lingered so long over his cot, watching him gurgle and clench his tiny fists. Or perhaps she wanted to delay the inevitable meeting with Alvar.

She had seen him riding beside the King on his way to the cathedral today, and all her hard-won peace built over the past months had been shattered. One look at his stern, unsmiling face had brought back all the pain she had banished from her heart. While Alvar was gone Elspeth had managed to reconcile herself to living at court, even finding some real happiness in helping to care for the tiny prince.

Although she searched the crowded room with her eyes, she could see no sign of him below. Perhaps he had already left the palace on some errand for His Majesty, Elspeth thought, pain mingling with relief. She dreaded the prospect of their next meeting, remembering how coldly he had refused to help her the last time they met. Why, oh why did her foolish heart start to beat more quickly at the very sight of him? How could she love a man who so obviously despised her?

Lost in her own thoughts, Elspeth was not aware of Philip Rathbone's approach. His voice made her jump. 'Are you not coming down to join the celebrations?' he asked, a wry note in his voice.

Elspeth gave him a slight smile. 'I did not see you, sir.'

'You were lost in your own thoughts, my lady. Why so sad?'

'I am not sad. This is a joyous day, is it not?'

'Perhaps.' The wry note was back in his voice. 'So Henry Tudor has his heir and we must all rejoice, even though he continues to slight his lady wife and her supporters.'

Elspeth looked at him anxiously. 'Hush, sir. Have a care lest your words reach the wrong ears.'

Philip shrugged his shoulders, frowning. Then his frown disappeared as he saw her anxious look. 'Do not be anxious for me, Lady Elspeth. I know when to be cautious, but I also know I can trust you.' He smiled at her. 'You must be aware of how much I value your good opinion. I have wanted to say more—but I have thought your heart lay elsewhere . . .'

Elspeth felt the hot colour stain her cheeks. 'I do not know what you mean.'

Philip took her hand impulsively. 'Can it be that you do not know how much I love you? Surely not!'

'I—I was aware of your friendship,' Elspeth whispered, unable to meet his eyes. 'But I did not believe it was more than that . . .'

'You cannot have thought that!' Philip cried, his eyes glowing with a new excitement. 'You have prevented me from speaking a score of times. If that be not true, then let me speak now. Let me ask you to be my wife.'

Elspeth stared at him, feeling confused. How had this happened? She had not meant him to declare himself. It was a way of escape, but did she want to take it? She liked Philip as a friend, but she was not sure she could learn to love him. And yet she had been prepared to marry a suitor of her aunt's choice, knowing that the man she loved could never return her love. What other choice was there for her? As Philip's wife she could leave the court—and then she would never be tempted to lose herself in Alvar's embrace again. Then, perhaps, she would be able to forget him.

Elspeth drew a deep breath. 'Even if I were to consent, sir, the King would never give his permission. He must know of your friendship with the Queen-Dowager through his spies. You are the last person he would let me wed—a known Yorkist sympathiser!'

Philip laughed. 'The King is not all-powerful, lady. If I could find a way—would you consent to wed me without his consent?'

Elspeth paled. 'He would have us thrown into prison. Nowhere in England would be safe for us.'

Philip hesitated, choosing his words carefully. 'It

might be that we should need to leave England for a time—until circumstances alter and we can return.'

Elspeth glanced anxiously over her shoulder, afraid of being overheard. This was treason! For a moment she was tempted to take the chance of escape he was offering her; then she realised she could not do it. 'It is not possible,' she said, a note of regret in her voice. 'My brothers are the King's wards, and they might suffer if I disobeyed him. I will not be the cause of their disgrace—or even their deaths.'

He laid his hand on her arm. 'Supposing you were just to disappear and no one knew what had become of you? Your brothers could not be blamed, and His Majesty would soon cease to search for you.'

Elspeth shook her head. 'No, it cannot be. I am honoured that you should want me as your wife, and I think we might have found contentment together—but we must put all such thoughts from our minds.'

Philip was silent, hiding his annoyance at her stubbornness. For a long time now he had been making plans—plans which included the Earl of Murran's daughter. It would have made things much easier if she had agreed to a marriage between them, but her refusal was merely another obstacle to be overcome. The Lady Elspeth was a small but essential part of his schemes, neither her feelings nor the lives of her brothers could be allowed to stand in his way. When the time came she would do as she was told, but for now she must suspect nothing.

He kissed her hand. 'Then I shall say no more, my lady, for I would never willingly bring grief to you.'

Elspeth smiled. 'I hope we can still be friends?'

'Of course.' He released her hand. 'And now, I beg you will excuse me.'

Elspeth nodded, watching for a moment as he walked away, noticing he made no attempt to join the other courtiers in the hall below. She sighed, half regretting her decision to reject his offer of marriage. It was probably the only chance she would ever have of finding some kind of happiness—but she had no choice. She dare not disobey the King so flagrantly.

Realising it was time she went down to join the celebrations, Elspeth moved from behind a huge stone pillar and began to walk slowly down the stairs. She was unaware of Alvar's eyes watching her, and she did not know that he had observed her meeting with Philip Rathbone.

Moving through the crowded hall, Elspeth joined the other ladies in attendance on the Queen. They were laughing at the antics of a troupe of tumblers; and Elspeth noticed the sad dwarf who had entertained the court at Westminster. She saw him looking at her and smiled briefly as she passed.

The Queen clapped her hands as the performance ended, sending the tumblers away. Then she turned to look at Elspeth inquiringly. 'How is my son?' she asked, a sweet smile lighting her pretty face.

Elspeth curtsied to her. 'He is well, Your Majesty. I watched him until he fell asleep.'

The Queen nodded. 'He is a handsome child, is he not? A worthy prince for England.'

'He is beautiful,' Elspeth agreed. 'As fair a babe as I have ever seen.'

'His Majesty is pleased with his son,' the Queen said, looking happy.

'He could not fail to be pleased, Your Majesty,' replied Elspeth, knowing her mistress was happy because the King was at last spending some time with her.

The Queen smiled at her. 'You were made for motherhood, Lady Elspeth—one day you will have sons of your own. Go and find some handsome gentleman to dance with you. Your duties are finished for this evening.'

Elspeth felt herself blushing. She curtsied to her mistress, moving towards the overhanging gallery where the minstrels had begun to play. Laughing couples had already joined hands to form sets for a lively country dance; and a young man asked Elspeth to dance.

She shook her head. 'Forgive me, sir. I do not feel like dancing for the moment. I would rather watch if you do not mind.'

The youth looked disappointed, but after a moment he approached another of the Queen's ladies and was accepted. Elspeth was momentarily alone as she watched the dancers.

'Do you not dance this evening, lady?'

Elspeth felt her flesh tingle with little pinpricks of ice, making her shiver all over as she recognised the voice and spun round, finding herself gazing up into Alvar's cold blue eyes. Then a strange thing happened as they looked at each other. His eyes lost their coldness and he smiled at her.

'Well—have you nothing to say to me?' he asked, a new, teasing note in his voice.

Elspeth dragged her eyes from his, fighting for calm. She must not give herself away, though her heart was beating so loudly he could surely hear it! 'It is a long time since we met, my lord. I hope you are well.'

Alvar laughed. 'How polite you are, Lady Elspeth. I thought you would be ready to fly at my throat.'

Elspeth clenched her hands at her sides. She would not let him make her angry. It was safer to show no emotion. 'Indeed, I was disappointed when we last parted—but I did not blame you for refusing to help me,' she said carefully, avoiding his eyes. 'It was selfish of me to ask such a favour. After all, why should you risk offending His Majesty for my sake?'

Alvar frowned. 'I had not thought to find you so understanding—especially as I was wrong.'

Elspeth wrinkled her brow. 'Wrong? I do not follow you, sir. I was at fault. I should not have asked you for help.'

'Who else could you ask?' A wry smile played about

Alvar's mouth. 'Not Philip Rathbone, I trust. You do not believe he could help you—do you?'

Elspeth's head shot up, her eyes narrowing suspiciously. 'Why should I think that?'

A guarded look crept into Alvar's eyes. 'You would do well not to become too close a friend of Mr Rathbone, Lady Elspeth—particularly if you want His Majesty to look kindly on your request to visit your sister.'

Elspeth's eyes opened wide with shock. She felt the colour drain from her face and her hands began to tremble. 'Oh, pray do not tease me, my lord,' she whispered, her heart beating so wildly that she could hardly breathe.

Alvar laughed softly, the look in his eyes making her knees turn to water. 'Why do you stare at me so, lady? Do you not believe me?'

Elspeth took a step forward, forgetting that she meant to keep her distance from him. Her eyes were dark and glowing as she gazed up at him earnestly. 'Is it really so?' she asked eagerly. 'Have you really spoken to His Majesty on my behalf? Oh, what did he say? Tell me! Tell me at once!'

'But perhaps you have changed your mind?' Alvar teased, unable to resist mocking her a little. 'Perhaps you no longer want my help?'

Elspeth gave a little gurgle of laughter. This was Alvar as she had dreamt he could be; gently teasing, his eyes no longer cold but full of laughter—and something else. Pray God she wasn't dreaming!

'Wretch that you are!' she cried, forgetting all caution in a dizzy surge of happiness. 'You shall tell me. You shall!'

Alvar relented. 'I took advantage of His Majesty's mellow mood—he has consented. I am to escort you to your sister's on my way to London. I shall leave you there while I complete my business, and then we will return together. You should have at least two weeks with Lady Nanette—mayhap longer if I can delay our return for a time.'

'Oh . . .' Elspeth pressed her hands together, gazing up at him in delight. 'I can hardly believe it. I am so happy! How can I ever thank you, my lord?'

Alvar smiled down at her. 'I want no thanks, my lady.' He hesitated for a moment, seeming almost awkward. 'You once offered me friendship and I refused it. Dare I ask you to forgive me?'

Elspeth stared at him in amazement. Could this really be the proud, cold Lord Alvar? He sounded almost humble as he asked for her friendship—how could this be the same man who had forced her into submission, crushing her resistance with a brutal passion? What could have wrought such a change in him?

Gazing up into his face, Elspeth thought she knew. Only love could work such a miracle. Alvar loved her. He must have discovered it, as she had, at their last meeting. His pride had kept him from admitting it then, but the long months apart had taught him to accept it. How much it must be costing him now to ask for her forgiveness!

Elspeth held out her hand to him, giving him a smile of such rare sweetness that only a monster could have remained unmoved. 'I should be honoured to count myself your friend, my lord.'

Alvar took the hand she offered, lifting it to his lips to kiss it briefly, sending tiny tremors of pleasure through Elspeth's entire body. She was so happy that she could not stop smiling at him, even though the new warmth in his eyes made her a little shy. The way he looked at her brought a fresh colour to her cheeks, and she thought that if they were alone he would not be content to kiss her hand. And in that moment Elspeth knew she could conceive of no greater happiness than to be Alvar's wife. She cared not if all the tales told of him were true. Nothing mattered but that he should love her as she loved him.

Alvar held out his hand to her, his strong, brown fingers curling about her slender, white ones. 'Will you dance with me, Elspeth?' he asked softly, his eyes lingering on her lovely face.

'Yes—oh, yes, my lord,' Elspeth replied, gazing up at him with glowing eyes.

She smiled up at him trustingly, forgetting all the pain his coldness had caused her as she basked in the warmth of his smiles.

Two weeks later Elspeth left Winchester for her sister's house, escorted by Alvar and some twenty men-at-arms. Lord Alvar never travelled without his own trusted retainers; for despite the end of the wars between the houses of Lancaster and York the roads were still haunted by bands of roving beggars and thieves. Many an unwary traveller found himself stripped of all his goods and left by the roadside, sometimes to die of his wounds before help came.

However, Elspeth's journey was uneventful. She had brought Nessie with her, but this time she did not need to be guarded from Alvar. If he had come to her room during the nights they slept at various inns on their route, Elspeth might have been tempted to send Nessie away; but he did not come. He treated her with a gentle courtesy which enchanted her. This was a new Alvar, and one she found irresistible. She had loved him in spite of his cruel words and harsh manner, now she was charmed by his almost tender care for her comfort.

So far Alvar had not asked her to be his wife, but he was paying court to her, of that she had no doubt. His manner was that of a lover with his betrothed. She delighted in his gentle teasing, the special way he looked at her which made her feel she was precious to him, thrilling to the touch of his hands as he helped her to mount her palfrey. Sometimes he would mention his home as they rode together, and Elspeth thought she could hear an aching longing in his voice as he told of the wild beauty of mountains and valleys, and of the forest in which he hunted as a young man.

'I would like to see your home,' she said shyly one morning, glancing at him from beneath her thick, curling lashes, a touch of colour in her cheeks.

Alvar frowned and Elspeth sensed a tenseness in him as he said: 'Perhaps you will one day.'

Somehow he seemed reluctant to speak of his home now, and Elspeth knew she should have let the subject drop, but she was curious. For though he told her of the glorious countryside surrounding Alvar Manor, he never mentioned the house or the people who lived there.

'Why do you not return to Alvar Manor?' she asked. 'Do you not long to be at home?'

'Sometimes.' He shrugged his shoulders, and Elspeth saw a fleeting quiver of pain about his mouth. 'But even if I wanted to leave the court I could not go without Henry's permission. I am as much a prisoner as you, Elspeth. I am bound by my promise to the King. I must and will serve him for as long as he needs me. This peace of ours is a tenuous one. There are many who seek to thrust Henry Tudor from the throne and replace him with another.'

Elspeth wrinkled her brow thoughtfully. 'I know some of the Yorkist nobles are dissatisfied with their lot—but would they really rise against His Majesty now that he has an heir? Surely that would also work against the Queen and her son—and she has the strongest claim to the throne.'

Alvar's face was stern. 'There are others who could claim an almost equal right to wear the crown—the young Earl of Warwick, for instance.'

'But he is only a child—and Henry has him locked away in the Tower.' Elspeth looked at Alvar. 'I saw the Earl once some years ago. He stayed at Murran Castle for a few days—that was before King Richard decided to imprison him at Sherriff Hutton. The poor boy, what a miserable life he has had. First Richard's prisoner, and now Henry Tudor's.'

Alvar frowned. 'Life can be cruel, Elspeth. I too am sorry for the boy—but if Henry allowed him his freedom, others would use him for their own ends.'

'Yes, I suppose so.' Elspeth sighed. 'It was his misfortune to be born a prince in such troubled times.'

'Henry can be merciful if he chooses. Perhaps he will let the lad live in exile when he feels himself more secure.'

Elspeth nodded. 'Pray God it may be so.' She glanced at him quickly. 'Perhaps you will be free to return to Alvar then, my lord?'

'Perhaps.' Alvar looked pensive. 'It might be that I shall beg Henry's indulgence to spend a few weeks at the manor when my business in London is finished. I have been absent for more than three years—it is time I went back . . .'

His voice sounded rather odd and Elspeth studied his face, alarmed to see the cold light in his eyes. 'Does something trouble you, my lord?' she asked. 'Is there some secret sorrow in your heart—something to do with your home?'

He looked startled. 'Why do you ask?' he demanded, his voice harsh. 'What have you heard?'

'Why—nothing . . .' Elspeth faltered. 'I am sorry if I have offended you, my lord. I meant no harm.'

Alvar smiled wryly. 'It is I who should ask for forgiveness—I jumped to the attack with no cause. And just when I had hoped you might learn to trust me. Do you trust me, Elspeth?'

'Why, yes, my lord. I think you know my heart, sir—but I am not sure of yours.'

Alvar laughed harshly, a bleak expression in his eyes. 'I have no heart, Elspeth. It was cut out of me a long time ago.'

Elspeth shook her head. 'I do not believe that, though

I can see you have suffered some deep grief. Will you not tell me about it?'

'It is an old wound, Elspeth—nothing that need concern you.' He was silent for a moment, obviously deep in thought, then: 'If I could gain Henry's consent to a marriage between us—would you marry me, Elspeth? Would you come back to Alvar with me?'

Elspeth felt the warm colour sweeping up into her cheeks, and her heart thundered in her breast. It was what she wanted, yet now he asked she was suddenly afraid. What had caused that bleak look in his eyes? He was looking at her now as she hesitated, that wry mockery curling his mouth as though he could read her thoughts.

'I will not press you for an answer, Elspeth,' he said, and there was an underlying sadness in his voice which tore at her heart. 'Soon we shall be at your sister's house. I will leave you there and you shall have time to consider your answer.'

Elspeth was silent. She wanted to cry out that she loved him and would wed him this instant if he wished it, but something held her back. She found herself suddenly prey to all kinds of doubts. How could she be sure he loved her? He was so unpredictable, changing his moods as the changing winds. One minute cold and stern, the next her tender lover. What manner of man was he? Why should he pretend to care for her if he did not?

The answer came unbidden, like a slithering serpent worming its unwelcome way into her mind. She smothered it immediately, unwilling to believe it, wanting to recapture the shimmering happiness which had been hers for so brief a time. Alvar had asked her to be his wife, and she wanted that so very much, but the tiny seed of doubt had taken root and she could not quite pluck it out.

Was it possible that the change in Alvar was due not to his love of Elspeth—but to her Aunt Ursula's fortune?

She remembered the cruel words he had once said to her:

'Why should I wed you? You have no name, no fortune . . .'

She swept the ugly suspicion from her mind. She would not let it poison her thoughts. If she once let the doubts gain a hold on her they would fester like a gangrenous wound, eventually destroying her. She loved Alvar and she trusted him. She must trust him or she was lost!

She looked at him. 'You shall have my answer when you return,' she said.

CHAPTER SEVEN

It was mid afternoon when the little cavalcade finally reached High Meadows, the home of Sir Harold Fitzwilliam and his lady wife; and the shadows of a wintry sun were filling the paved courtyard where the couple waited to greet their guests.

Elspeth immediately noticed the change in Sir Harold; from a stout, healthy man, he had withered away into a bent and greying wreck of humanity. And his suffering was mirrored in Nanette's gentle eyes as she came to clasp her sister in loving arms. For a moment they clung wordlessly, tears mingling as their cheeks touched. Then Nanette let her go and Elspeth held out her hands to her brother-in-law, seeing the true welcome in his eyes. He patted her shoulder awkwardly, then drew her into a warm embrace.

'Welcome, sister,' he said. 'Welcome indeed. I know how much this day means to my dearest Nan.' Looking up at his cousin, who had not dismounted, he said: 'How can we thank you for bringing her to us, Alvar?'

Alvar smiled slightly. 'Do not speak of thanks, cousin. I need none.'

Nanette glanced up at him as his horse moved restlessly. 'Will you not break your journey? Will you not spend the night with us—or at least stay to refresh yourself? We would both be honoured to have you beneath our roof, my lord.'

Alvar's smile deepened as he met her gentle look, his face losing the strained expression it had been wearing a few minutes earlier. 'Would that I were able, Lady Nanette. My business is urgent and will not wait while I pleasure myself in your company—but I will accept your hospitality when I return, that I promise you.'

Elspeth moved to Nanette's side, gazing up at him with eyes which reflected her emotions more truly than she realised, so that he saw the mixture of regret and relief she felt at this parting. A black mood had hung over him for the last part of their journey, and few words had passed between them. He leaned down to take the hand Elspeth offered, clasping it briefly, his eyes faintly reproachful—or was that merely her imagination? Alvar could not guess the doubts which had tortured her since he had asked her to be his wife.

'I wish you a fair journey, my lord,' she said, colour staining her cheeks as she remembered another leave-taking.

Alvar smiled, a hint of mockery in his face as though he too was recalling that day at Murran Castle. 'I shall not return too soon, lady,' he said, a harsh note in his voice. 'I know how much this visit means to you. I would not want to end it too quickly—though I shall be impatient for your answer.'

Elspeth's throat felt hot and tight and tears stung her eyes, but she would not let them fall. Though her heart cried out that he could have his answer now, her tongue seemed glued to the roof of her mouth. She did not understand the mood which had held him silent these many miles. She could not guess what brought those haunted shadows to his eyes, nor why he had withdrawn from her so suddenly.

She stood in the walled courtyard of Nanette's home, watching with her sister and Sir Harold as Alvar rode out at the head of his men. Her throat ached with the effort of holding back her emotion, and she hardly knew she had spoken until she heard her own voice cry out: 'Alvar!'

The cry was so hoarse that she thought he could not possibly hear it; but he turned in the saddle as though he had been waiting for some sign from her, his eyes seeking hers with an intentness which bored deep into her soul. Then he lifted his hand in brief salute.

Elspeth trembled as for an instant she knew an urgent desire to run after him and confess her love before it was too late. But her ankles were hobbled by invisible bonds. She stilled the madness in her blood, relaxing a little as she felt Nanette's arm steal round her waist.

Nothing had changed, she realised. She was to spend two weeks with her beloved sister, and then Alvar would return. He would demand an answer from her, an answer that she had already given in her heart. She turned away from his receding figure as Nanette drew her gently towards the house.

Nanette was smiling at her, a smile full of understanding that asked no questions. 'You cannot know how much I have longed to have you here with me—with us, Elspeth. Harold has hoped for it too, for all our sakes. He is truly fond of you, my dear.' She squeezed her sister's waist affectionately. 'It seems so long since we were children together in the castle, though it is scarcely more than three years—but you are no longer a child . . .'

'No—I am not a child any more.' Elspeth raised her lovely eyes to her sister's face, love driving away the shadows which had turned them almost black. 'I have thought of this day so often, Nan. I have wanted to visit you and Sir Harold so desperately—and now I am here at last. We must make the most of this precious time. We must not waste a second!' She returned her sister's hug. 'Oh, dearest, dearest Nan, tell me all your news!'

The days continued cold and bright; the wintry sun bringing a false impression of summer as the leaves began to wither and fall, leaving the trees stark and bare against a white sky. But ensconced in the comfort of the manor house, which seemed almost small after the echoing vastness of the palace, Elspeth basked in the warmth of her sister's love; and gradually the tension eased out of her. The aching loneliness of the past three years was soothed away by Nanette's tender care, and it was almost as if they had never been apart.

Their days passed in quiet contentment. Nanette was a good wife to her husband; and her household ran smoothly, providing every comfort. She took pride in seeing that everything was well ordered, waxing the heavy oak furniture herself, though she had servants at her bidding. Her husband sometimes scolded her mildly for working so hard; but Nanette enjoyed the feel of the smooth wood beneath her hands, just as she liked to see the neat pots of preserves on the shelves in her stillroom.

Elspeth's wild spirit was temporarily lulled by the peace of her sister's home, and there were times when she almost envied her obvious contentment, which was marred only by Sir Harold's ill-health and their lack of a child. She found herself growing wistful, her thoughts straying to a future as Alvar's wife. Was it possible that she could ever find the same contentment in such a marriage?

One day as the sisters were sitting before the open fire, busy with their stitching and talking of nothing in particular, Elspeth looked across at Nanette, unaware of the wistful look in her eyes as she said: 'Do you remember telling me that Alvar was not as wicked as I believed, Nan?'

Nanette nodded. 'Yes.' She laid down her needlework, her mouth curving in a soft smile as she saw the dreamy expression on her sister's face. 'I have good reason to know it. Things would have gone hard with us these past few months if it had not been for Lord Alvar. He refuses to speak of it, and he will not be thanked—but he has done much for Harold.'

Elspeth pricked her finger, sucking the blood to cover her confusion. 'I—I think he means to ask me to marry him,' she said, her eyes suddenly sweeping up to Nanette's. 'How should I answer him?'

Nanette sighed, somehow she had guessed what was

in her sister's mind. 'You love him—don't you?'

'Yes—but . . .'

'But what, my dear? If you love him that should be enough for you. Do not demand too much of life, Elspeth, you only hurt yourself. Have a little patience. Lord Alvar is a difficult man to understand—but I think there is goodness in him.'

Elspeth laughed wryly. 'You would seek to find virtue in the Devil himself.' She looked into her sister's gentle face appealingly, her eyes growing dark with passion. 'Do you think he could come to love me?'

'I think he might.' Nanette's smile was mildly teasing. 'But you have already made up your mind to marry him—haven't you?'

Elspeth drew a long, sighing breath. 'Sometimes I am so sure—and then I wonder if I am a silly little fool to be taken in by his handsome face . . .'

Nanette frowned. 'It might help if you knew Alvar's story.' She hesitated, obviously wanting to speak. 'Harold is resting now and I do not like to disturb him, but I will talk to him before supper and ask his permission to tell you the truth.'

Elspeth sighed. She felt that nothing Nan could tell her would solve her problem, since all she wished to know of Alvar was that he truly loved her. Nothing else really mattered. She wished that she had had the courage to ask him why he wanted to marry her, and what he had meant by his mysterious remark: 'I have no heart. It was cut out of me a long time ago.' Surely if he really cared for her it would not have been too hard to make him confess it! But she had been afraid to look too deeply into the heart of the man she loved.

She stood up impatiently, a restless mood taking hold of her. 'I think I shall go for a ride before supper, Nan. I do not suppose you care to come with me?'

Nanette shook her head. 'I ride only when I have to, my dear. I never had your fondness for it.' She got up and walked to the window, looking out at the sky. 'It will soon be getting dark—are you sure you want to go?'

'Yes. I shall not be long, Nan. A few minutes to change my gown; a brisk canter as far as the mill pond and then home again. I have a headache and the fresh air will do me good.'

'As you wish.' Nanette sighed, knowing that wild look in Elspeth's face of old. 'But you will take a groom with you?'

'Yes, of course.' Elspeth kissed her sister's cheek impulsively. 'Do not worry so much. What harm could come to me here?'

Nanette smiled at her fondly. 'None. The villagers are all good, honest folk, and they respect Harold—but still it is only seemly that you take a groom with you.'

'And so I will—do not fuss, dearest. I am not the madcap child I used to be.'

Elspeth laughed and sped out of the room, her mood lifting as she ran up the wide staircase and along the passage to her chamber. Less than fifteen minutes later she was dressed in a simple grey riding gown and on her way to the stables. Lady Nanette had sent a servant on ahead of her, and a chestnut mare was ready saddled, while a groom waited patiently to accompany her. Elspeth smiled to herself: Nanette was taking no chances!

The groom helped her to mount, and together they set off across the fields. The ground was hard beneath their horses' hooves, for it had not rained these past three weeks; and the soft thud was music to Elspeth's ears. This was the freedom she had so sorely missed during her months of semi-imprisonment in the palace. The sweet scent of crushed grass filled her nostrils; the sting of wind in her face brought a fresh colour to her cheeks, and her spirit soared as she saw the open spaces unfolding before her.

The mill was soon reached. Elspeth paused for a moment, watching the heavy wooden sails and the huge wheel churning relentlessly through the muddy waters of the pond. She was reluctant to return so soon; her appetite had merely been whetted and she felt the need for a longer gallop. It was only another mile or so to the village and the crossroads; from there she could see the road which eventually led to London. The road Alvar had taken almost two weeks earlier.

She turned the mare's head sharply, not bothering to look over her shoulder to make sure the groom was following; but she could hear the steady clop of hooves behind her. The light was fading rapidly as they passed the village, and the sky seemed leaden as though a storm was brewing. Elspeth reined in as she reached the crossroads, halting her horse in the middle of the road, her eyes straining in the direction of the Capital, as if her longing would suddenly conjure up a band of horsemen out of nowhere.

At first she thought the sound of rattling coachwheels and flying hooves was only her imagination, a product of her wistful thoughts; then she realised that the sound came from behind her. She glanced over her shoulder, growing alarmed as she saw a coach drawn by six horses coming towards her very quickly. Abandoning her dreams, she dug her heels into the mare's flank sharply, knowing she must move fast or be crushed by the on-rush of the coach; but even as she did so, an owl screeched from close by, startling her horse and causing the animal to rear up wildly. Elspeth was thrown as the mare bolted, landing with a sickening thud in the path of the on-coming coach.

For a few seconds the world seemed to go black, and she did not hear her groom's frantic yells, nor see the driver of the coach tugging furiously at his horses' reins as he somehow pulled them to a shuddering halt inches from her sprawled figure. At once Elspeth's groom had dismounted and rushed to her side, to be followed moments later by the occupant of the coach.

'My mistress is hurt,' the groom said, looking up at the gentleman anxiously.

'By my faith—the Lady Elspeth!' the fair-haired stranger cried, and the groom gaped at him in open-mouthed astonishment.

'Do you know the Lady Elspeth, sir?' he asked.

'Why, yes, man. I am a good friend of the lady's—we met at court. Quick, help me to carry her to my coach. I fear she may be badly hurt.'

But even as he spoke, Elspeth stirred and opened her eyes, blinking and groaning as she found herself gazing up into the anxious faces of her groom and Philip Rathbone. 'Philip?' she muttered in bewilderment. 'The coach . . . I was thrown . . .' She struggled into a sitting position, gasping as the world spun round in a mad kaleidoscope. 'Oh, my head hurts!'

'You certainly cannot ride in your condition, Lady Elspeth,' Philip said, bending over her, helping her as she rose unsteadily to her feet. 'Have you any pain? Let me help you to my carriage. I will take you to your sister's house.'

Elspeth smiled at him, grateful for the support of his arm around her, and not yet wondering how he knew she was staying with Nanette. 'Thank you. I am sorry to take you out of your way, sir, but I do not believe I could ride my horse at the moment.'

'I will not hear of you attempting it.' Philip Rathbone turned to the groom hovering beside them awkwardly. 'Fetch your mistress's horse, sirrah, and ride on ahead to let them know we are coming!'

'Yes, sir.'

The man sprang into action, relieved to have his orders. He mounted his own horse and set off in pursuit of the mare, who had halted her mad flight and was standing, ears pricked, some little way off.

Philip eased Elspeth into the coach, placing a silk cushion at her back and a warm coverlet over her lap, all the while murmuring little noises of tender concern. Then he took his seat beside her, drawing the heavy velvet curtains across the open doorway of the carriage to keep out the chill of the night air and the tiny spots of rain which were beginning to fall.

Elspeth felt a lurch as the horses started to move, her aching body crying out in protest as the coach swayed dangerously, making a half circle to return the way it had come. She sighed and leaned her head against the wooden strut supporting the arched roof of the carriage, her temples beginning to throb as the unwieldy coach jolted over the uneven road.

Philip leant towards her, an anxious expression in his eyes as he saw her pale face. 'Are you ill, my lady? Where is the pain?'

Elspeth stifled a groan, trying to smile at him, but not succeeding very well. 'My head . . . I think . . .' She pressed her hands to her temples as the faintness washed over her again and the world seemed to spin round.

Philip pushed something into her hands. 'Here—drink this, Lady Elspeth, it will ease your pain.'

Elspeth blinked, staring at the tiny vial of dark liquid as the throbbing, purple lights crashed in her head. 'What is it?' she asked, her voice shaking almost as much as her hands.

'A simple cordial, lady, nothing more.' The soothing tone of Philip's voice comforted her. 'Come—I will help you. Swallow it all, it cannot harm you.'

He held her trembling hand firmly in his own, forcing it up so that the vial was at her lips. She gulped the contents down obediently, hardly tasting the slight bitterness. Flashes of white and purple lights were exploding inside her head, and an iron band seemed to be crushing her temples. She felt so ill that it was a relief to let herself relax against Philip's shoulder as he slipped his arm around her waist.

'Close your eyes and try to relax,' he said, his voice soft and seductively soothing. 'You know you have nothing to fear while I am with you.'

Elspeth found that she could do nothing but obey him. She was feeling very strange. The pain in her temples was easing, just as he had promised, but the faintness seemed to be increasing. Her eyelids were growing heavy, and everything was becoming hazy. Her limbs felt limp and useless, as though they were no longer at her command. It was an effort to keep her eyes open.

'Go to sleep, my lady,' Philip's voice had taken on a note of command beneath the silkiness. 'Do not fight it—it will be easier for you.'

Somewhere a warning bell sounded in Elspeth's brain as she struggled to remember something. She knew it was important: something Philip had known she had not told him. But the effort was too much for her, even to speak was impossible, her lips felt thick and swollen. From deep within her a primeval instinct made her fight against the creeping sloth which was taking possession of her body. But it was already too late, for even as she struggled to move away from him, the invidious blackness closed in upon her senses, robbing her of all conscious thought.

Elspeth's head moved restlessly on the pillow, a deep sighing sob escaping her cracked lips. Her eyelids flickered against her hot cheeks, and her hands clutched feverishly at the restricting coverlets as she moaned out loud. Her gummed eyelids seemed too heavy to open and she sank back into unconsciousness, unaware of the watching figures around her bed.

A day and a night passed while Elspeth lay in her drugged sleep, and it was night again when at last her eyes opened. She lay staring into the thick blackness around her, tasting the dry bitterness on her tongue, her mind numbed and blank. She had no pain, but for the moment she could not remember where she was, nor what had happened to her. She seemed to have been ill—but where was she? Not in her chamber at Murran Castle; the bed she was lying in was too comfortable, and she had left the castle for some reason. Thoughts came and went in her mind, like wisps of mist floating across the moors. It was almost too much effort to chase after them, to make them fit together so that they made a pattern. Nanette's face floated into her vision, looking anxious.

'It will be getting dark—are you sure you want to go?'

'Nanette . . .' she croaked, but the vision faded. She struggled to remember—there was something about Nanette, something to do with her visit to Nanette. She had been riding . . .

It was instinct and not conscious thought that made her stiffen as she heard muffled voices and the grating of a key in a lock—why was she locked in? A door swung open on squeaking hinges, and there was the sound of heavy feet on wooden floors. Not knowing why she did so, but obeying some primitive intuition for survival, Elspeth closed her eyes as the curtains were swished back from around her bed, willing her eyelids not to flicker as she felt the heat from a candle flame thrust close to her face.

'She's still sleeping,' a voice said, rising on a note of annoyance. 'In God's name!—what made you do it, Philip? If he discovered she was here in London, and your prisoner, he would show you no mercy—be sure of that!'

There was a slight pause, then another voice which stirred in Elspeth's memory, bringing back the missing pieces of the puzzle with startling clarity. 'It was a heaven-sent opportunity, Markham, I couldn't resist it. There was I, scheming how best to steal her away from her sister's house and she just fell into my hands like a ripe plum—and after I thought all was lost! I had hoped to persuade her to an elopement, but she proved more stubborn that I imagined—then he started to meddle in my affairs and carried her off for some devious plan of his own. I think he means to have her himself . . .'

'I still say it was foolish,' the first voice replied. 'What use will she be to you if she is unwilling? As the Earl of Murran's daughter, she could win much support for our cause—but not if she refuses to accept the boy.'

'She was a mere child when the Earl of Warwick visited her father's castle—if I tell her Lambert Simnel is the Earl, she will have no reason to doubt me. I tell you, Markham, the girl is half in love with me already.'

'And what if she changes her mind after the way you have treated her? I doubt she'll take kindly to being drugged and abducted.'

Philip Rathbone laughed unpleasantly and Elspeth could barely repress the shudder that went through her; but fortunately for her, he was looking at Markham and did not notice the slight trembling of her hands.

'She will forgive me when I tell her I acted on impulse—because I was desperate for love of her. I shall throw myself at her feet and beg her to forgive me—her vanity will not allow her to think differently—and if she does not forgive . . .' there was a significant pause. 'I shall have to persuade the lady a little less kindly. When I have had her in my bed a few times she will beg me to marry her, and then . . .'

'And then you will be master of both the lady and her considerable fortune.' Markham made a sound of distaste in his throat. 'I almost pity her. I think she will not find you an easy master. Beneath that pretty face of yours, Philip, you are a ruthless swine.'

Philip Rathbone laughed, sounding highly amused. 'Getting squeamish, Markham? Have you forgotten our cause? Or is it that you begin to love the Tudor dog?'

The other man swore harshly. 'Damn you, Rathbone! You know I have no love for Henry Tudor. I do not forget his insults to the House of York—nor the way Stafford met his death. I served him faithfully as I serve Burgundy now. I shall not rest until the throne of England lies in worthier hands. No, I do not forget, but the girl is merely a pawn in the game. I would have had her willing help if it were possible, not this wickedness you plan. I pray you, treat her gently—if only for her father's sake.'

Philip laughed again. 'Content you, sir. I will kiss away her fears—unless she defies me too long.'

Markham shivered as he heard the note of steel beneath the honeyed tone of Philip's voice. Bending over Elspeth, he peered into her face anxiously. 'She is very pale—are you sure you did not give her too much of that vile stuff you carry with you? What was it anyway—some devilry you brought back from your travels, I suppose?'

Philip's only answer was a harsh laugh, and Elspeth schooled herself to lie still as she felt the touch of a cool hand on her brow, refusing to let herself think about what she had just heard. She must stay calm! She must let them go on believing she was still asleep, if only to gain a little time. Strong fingers closed around her wrist suddenly and she moved involuntarily, her heart racing as the fingers seemed to hesitate, then exert a slight pressure, as if in warning.

'Her pulse is weak. I think I should send my physician to her. It will do you no good if she dies, Rathbone.'

'No, leave her be.' Philip's voice was hard, sending cold shivers through Elspeth so that it was all she could do not to jerk away as he bent over her himself. 'She won't die; I know what I am doing. She might feel a little ill when she wakes, that's all to the good. I shall tell her it was the result of her accident. But better she dies than that devil Alvar should hear of her presence here—remember she is in your house, Markham. I think he is already suspicious of me—and he wants her fortune for himself. When I learnt he meant to have her, I knew I must act quickly. I tried persuasion, but this is a surer way.'

'You are a cold devil,' Markham said, repressing a shudder.

'And you had rather not know me, but since you need me, you will force yourself to accept what I choose to do. Elizabeth Woodville was right when she warned me not to place too much faith in you. You surprise me,

Markham, I thought you made of sterner stuff!'

Markham's expression froze in the candlelight. 'I defy any man to call me coward,' he said angrily. 'But my stomach turns at what you plan. Well, she won't wake yet awhile, I warrant you. Come away now, man, you've more pressing business this night.'

'As you say—but it is a pity.' Philip sounded reluctant as he followed the other man to the door. 'She is beautiful, don't you think so, Markham? I am impatient for her awakening.' He chuckled. 'It will be a pleasure to break this particular filly. I almost hope she doesn't give in too easily.'

Markham's reply was lost as the solid oak door closed behind them and the key was securely turned again. Elspeth opened her eyes to a room that had been plunged into darkness once more, shivering, her mind now fully awake to the danger she was in. However, her natural fear was somewhat suppressed by a fierce anger. So Philip Rathbone thought to enjoy taming her, did he? Well, he would learn soon enough that she was no docile wench to be bent to his will! She would prefer death to a life as his tool after what she had heard tonight. So he believed she would beg for marriage? She would see him in Hell first!

Cautiously, her anger sustaining her as she felt the first pain from her aching limbs, she crept from the bed, her eyes straining to penetrate the gloom. Once she had parted the thick bed hangings, a thin shaft of moonlight through the narrow window showed her that she was in what appeared to be a comfortable bedchamber. For this she had Markham to thank, Elspeth guessed, since Philip Rathbone had shown no similar concern for her.

As her eyes grew accustomed to the dim light, Elspeth's gaze wandered round the room, sliding over the heavily-carved armoire and the oak coffer at the far end of the room. To the right of the armoire was the door through which the two men had just left, and near the small window was a table with a silver ewer and bowl set upon it. Then she gave a crow of delight as she saw her gown cast carelessly over a stool beside the bed. She was still wearing her petticoat and hose, something more she had to thank Markham for, she felt.

Conscious of the gritty heaviness of her eyelids and her throbbing head, she moved towards the silver ewer and bowl, each step jarring painfully. Lying in bed, she had not been aware of the bruises massing on her arms and legs, but now she could feel every one of them. Her head was hurting again, but it was not the blinding pain she had known when she was thrown, merely a dull throb, brought on by the foul stuff Philip Rathbone had given her to drink no doubt. He should pay for it if she paid too! Elspeth thought angrily. No matter what he did to her, she would not make it easy for him. Her fury helped to spur her on as the ground moved uneasily beneath her feet and she cursed her weakness. She paused for a moment, leaning on the edge of the table as a bout of faintness washed over her. Pray God there was water in that ewer!

The water swished against the metal sides of the jug as Elspeth lifted it to her parched lips, drinking eagerly, uncaring of the overspill which ran down her chin in cold tricklets. She gulped greedily, needing the salve of its coolness in her hot, aching throat; then, when she could drink no more, she poured the rest of the water into the bowl, scooping it up in her hands to splash her fevered skin. Bending down at last, she tore a strip from her petticoat and soaked it in the remaining water, pressing the cloth to her hot brow. Taking the cloth with her, Elspeth went to sit down on the edge of the bed once more.

Trailing its coolness over her neck and arms, she looked at the dark shape of her gown lying across the stool, thoughts of escape beginning to form in her brain. Why should she wait here tamely for Philip's return? Her face hardened with determination: somehow she was going to get out of her prison! Going down on her knees beside the bed, Elspeth groped in the darkness, giving a muffled cry of triumph as she found what she was looking for. She looked at her shoes for a moment before deciding not to put them on just yet; instead she struggled into her gown, wrestling with the laces at her bosom and thanking providence that she had not been wearing one of her more cumbersome gowns when Philip abducted her. Her hair was straggling about her shoulders, but there was nothing she could do about it, nor was this the time to be worrying about her appearance.

Shoes in hand, she walked silently across the wooden floor, still uncertain of what she was going to do next. She tried the door, turning the iron loop in a vain hope that it would open. It remained firmly closed; and Elspeth tugged at it in sudden, useless fury, as if she would force it open by the strength of her will. Her efforts were as effective as a trapped moth fluttering against a shuttered window. Exhausted, her head whirling from the strain, she leant against the door, trying not to give way to the tears building hotly behind her lids. Crying would not help her! What was she to do? The window was hardly more than a slit in the wall, too narrow for even her slender form to squeeze through. The only way out was through this door and it was locked. For a moment she thought wildly of hiding behind it and attacking whoever opened it next time, but she knew that such a plan was doomed to failure. Yet she had to get out before Philip returned. She had to! She would not wait tamely here for him, nor would she allow herself to be used in his plot against the King—whatever that might be; and she hadn't really understood a word of it.

She pressed her head close to the thick, oak door, willing herself to think of something. Suddenly she stiffened as she caught the sound of approaching footsteps. As the key scraped against the lock, she fled towards the huge armoire, shrinking back behind its shadow as the door opened. The flare of candlelight lit the room, and she saw two figures, a man and a woman, moving quietly in the direction of the bed.

'I think she was beginning to stir just now,' a voice said, and Elspeth recognised it as belonging to the man called Markham. 'I do not trust that devil Rathbone, and I'll not have her death on my conscience.' He reached out to draw back the bed hangings. 'See what you can do for her, Mary— What the . . . !'

Elspeth acted in the moment of his discovery. Running barefoot across the floor, she plunged through the open doorway, pulling the heavy door shut after her and locking it swiftly. The hall in which she found herself was quite dark, but there was a faint glow somewhere ahead of her. She ran towards the light, hearing a muffled shout from behind the stout door of the room she had just escaped from. The light was at the bottom of a short flight of stairs, one small candle set in an alcove. Pausing at the head of the stairs, Elspeth saw that she had only to cross a narrow passage to reach what looked like a street door.

Still clutching her shoes in her hand, Elspeth crept down the wooden stairs, her heart racing as she listened fearfully for any sign that her escape had been discovered. The door of her prison had been thick and any sounds from within would be muffled, with luck it would be a while before they were heard. As yet she had heard nothing more than the first startled shout as she locked the door. The thought crossed her mind that Markham might be giving her time to make good her escape before raising the alarm. She quickened her pace as she reached the bottom stair, hearing a door open somewhere at the rear of the house. Her feet flew across the short distance separating her from the outside door, praying that it was not locked.

Either the Almighty was listening or some careless servant had neglected his duty—or perhaps Markham had planned it so? The door swung open at her touch, revealing a paved courtyard. Not a street door then, but beyond the courtyard was another which almost certainly was. Not stopping to put on her shoes, Elspeth sped towards the far gate, finding this just as easy to open in its turn. Her escape had been made simple. Markham must have meant it so! She thanked God that her erstwhile host had such a care for his immortal soul.

Outside in the street, Elspeth paused to put on her shoes before plunging into headlong flight. The moon was full enough to show her that Markham's house was close by the river, and she followed its silver streak instinctively, knowing that her first concern was to put distance between herself and Philip Rathbone. On and on she ran, thinking only of the need to escape her captor, the fear she had suppressed earlier rising in her now as she let the panic flow over her.

Aching limbs were forgotten in her urgency; blind, unreasoning panic filled her mind as she ran, terror lending swiftness to her feat. On, ever on, into the dark loneliness of the night.

CHAPTER EIGHT

At last the ache in her breast became an unbearable pain, and Elspeth drew in a long, shuddering breath which hurt her lungs. Gasping for air she bent over double, hugging herself as she heard a roaring in her ears. After a moment she straightened up, dizzy and swaying on her feet, her heart thudding against her ribs as though it would burst from her body. Slowly the red mist cleared from her heated brain, leaving her calmer but bewildered.

She was dimly aware that she was lost, completely, utterly lost. She was somewhere in the City of London, she seemed to remember Markham saying that—but where? During her stay in the Capital Elspeth had seldom strayed from the small intimate world of the court; apart from her visits to Lady Ursula's house. Never before had she been alone in the city. Panic flared in her as she stared wildly into the darkness, but she fought it down, clinging to the thought which had sustained her from the moment she learned she was in London. Alvar was here. Somehow she had to find him.

Raising her head, Elspeth looked desperately for something which would help her—which way to turn? For several seconds she stared uncomprehendingly at the dark mass of rounded towers and spires outlined against the silver sky. Then she realised she was looking at the Tower of London itself. It was some distance ahead of her still, but if she could make her way there she knew she would be able to find help. It had been possible to see the Tower from the windows of Aunt Ursula's house: she was sure she could find her way to the house once she reached the fortress. One of her aunt's servants must surely know where Alvar lived!

Gathering her determination about her as she would a cloak, Elspeth began to walk towards the distant towers, following the curve of the river, her head bent against the rising wind. She felt a few drops of rain touch her face, but she stoically ignored them, just as she ignored the throbbing ache in her temples.

Sometimes she passed silent houses, their windows tightly shuttered against the night, and she was tempted to ask for help from the sleeping inmates, but caution held her back. She was very conscious of her unkempt hair and the mud clinging to the skirts of her gown. It had been raining at some time during the previous day and deep puddles lingered in the road, soaking through her thin shoes. She knew that if she dared to knock at one of the doors she would be sent away with angry abuse. They would think she was a harlot or worse—for what decent woman would roam the streets at this hour? No, her only hope was to find her aunt's house and make the servants let her in. Then she could send someone to Alvar. She refused to think about what might happen if the house had been closed and the servants dismissed. She had to go on!

She had been walking for some while, her thoughts firmly fixed on reaching the Tower and then Ursula's house, when she became uneasily aware that she was no longer alone. Small rustling sounds seemed to come from behind her. She paused, her heart thumping, spinning round suddenly to confront the dark, ragged shapes silently trailing her.

'Who are you?' Elspeth's voice was high with fear. 'What do you want?'

The ragged creatures sensed her fear. Becoming bolder, they advanced nearer, and she saw that beneath the foul rags they were really men, not demons of the night as she had at first feared. There were four of them in all, their faces grimed with filth, their bodies gaunt and starved.

'What do you want?' Elspeth asked again, hiding her trembling hands behind her back. 'Why are you following me? I have no money for you to steal.'

The creatures made no answer. Haunted eyes stared from deep, hollowed sockets, burning with a queer, insane fever as they devoured Elspeth's slender form. Habitual creatures of the darkness, they realised their prey was no ordinary woman of the streets. They stared at her as she stood at bay, the wind holding her gown taut about her thighs and slim hips, outlining the contours of her body.

She became aware of the cold and the wind where before she had thought only of reaching her destination. She shivered, her blood turning to ice-water in her veins as she gazed into the brutish, hungry faces. She felt as though her feet were nailed to the ground, and she knew that one false step would bring them down on her like a pack of wolves.

For an agonising eternity she stood unmoving, returning their silent menace with a cool pride which held them off. Then, as if the spell which held them in thrall had somehow broken, they began to move towards her, slowly and purposefully. Elspeth tensed, poised for flight. Fear rose in her throat to choke her. She smothered a sob, retreating backwards without daring to take her eyes from their faces.

Hearing a low growl issue as one from the four throats, Elspeth gave a scream of pure terror. Suddenly panic swept over her. She turned and fled, conscious of the pursuing feet and the animal noises behind her. All pretence of calm had deserted her now. She was sobbing with fear, stumbling in her haste. The heel of her shoe caught in a rut, causing her to pitch forward and fall heavily. She felt the sting of rough stone beneath her hands; it grazed her flesh and brought blood to the surface but she was not aware of the pain. Scrambling to her feet, she knew it was already too late—she was surrounded by four hideous, deathly-white faces, all leering at her with brutish lust.

'No!' she screamed, her eyes wide with horror. 'For pity's sake—no!'

Still none of the men spoke, though disgusting, animal grunts issued from their bloodless lips. Skinny hands poked at her, reaching out to stroke and squeeze; hands which ended in hooked, yellow talons. Then one of them grew bolder, grabbing a handful of her dark mane of curling hair, gibbering with excitement as Elspeth recoiled in terror. Another hand grasped the bodice of her gown, tearing eagerly as the thin material ripped apart in his fingers.

The sight of her white flesh seemed to send them crazy. Elspeth screamed as the foul-smelling bodies closed in on her. She went down beneath them, smothered by the sheer weight of four heaving, clawing bodies. Hands tore greedily at her clothing; the sound of rasping breathing filled her ears, blotting out all reason. She closed her eyes, trying to shut out the horror of what was happening to her. She screamed again, despairingly, knowing that no help could come to her.

The dark ball of fury came out of nowhere, exploding like a bolt of thunder in the midst of the scrambling bodies. Screams of agony rent the night as one of the beggars crawled away clutching his belly, blood streaming through his sprawled fingers. Suddenly the greedy hands fell away from Elspeth, and the horrible grunts stilled into an even more horrible silence.

Elspeth opened her eyes, looking blankly into the ugly face bending over her. She shivered, fearing she was about to be attacked again; then a small, wiry hand was held out to her in a gesture of help.

'You need be afraid no longer, my lady,' a voice said. 'These scum will not touch you again.'

Elspeth rose unsteadily to her feet, ignoring the dwarf's outstretched hand. She stared at him uncertainly, her eyes still dark with terror. 'I—I have seen you before,' she whispered, her voice shaking.

The dwarf bowed, forcing his twisted body into a semblance of elegance. 'Your servant, my lady. I told you I would remember you.' Suddenly he whirled on the silent beggars, fury shooting out of him like sparks from a blacksmith's anvil. 'Be gone, scum, or you will answer to me!'

'We didn't know she was yours, Quinn.' One of the ragged creatures spoke at last.

The dwarf jerked his head up, a dangerous light flickering in his bright eyes. 'Go!' he hissed, the note of command in his voice according ill with his stunted frame. But the ragged creatures began to slink away, disappearing into the shadows, carrying the wounded man with them.

Elspeth pressed her shaking fingers against her lips, holding back the hysterical laughter. Saved by a dwarf—a little pet no higher than her waist. It was ludicrous, ridiculous. She was trembling from head to foot, deep shudders forcing the breath out of her lungs in little, jerky sobs.

The dwarf watched, sensing the horror and pain which had brought her close to breaking point. His sad face filled with pity. 'Weep if it will help you, lady,' he said gently. 'No one but Quinn is here to see your tears—and Quinn is nobody at all.'

Elspeth shook her head, the shudders subsiding. 'You saved me,' she said wonderingly. 'Those creatures were afraid of you—who are you?'

Quinn gave her his sad smile. 'No one—nobody.' He held out his hand to her once more. 'Will you trust me, lady? I may be an ugly little monster—but inside I am as tall and straight as Lord Alvar . . .'

'Alvar!' Elspeth stared at him, suddenly eager. 'Do you know Lord Alvar? Do you know where I can find him?'

Quinn's hand sought and found Elspeth's, his fingers

closing comfortingly around hers. 'I will take you to him,' he promised. 'Trust me.'

Elspeth nodded wordlessly, letting him draw her on where he would. She clung to him, needing the reassurance of his touch, trusting blindly because she had no choice, no will of her own. She was numb now, unconscious of the heavy mud-soaked skirts of her gown clinging in tatters about her legs, aware only of the small figure trotting beside her on his short legs.

After what seemed like hours, but was in reality no more than thirty minutes, the dwarf halted. Elspeth stared at him stupidly, her dazed brain hardly realising why they had stopped. Quinn pointed to a large house just across the street from them. 'You will find Lord Alvar within,' he said. 'Go on alone, lady, I must leave you now.'

Elspeth stood uncertainly, staring at the house. 'Will you not come with me?' she asked, almost afraid to leave his protection. 'Alvar will see you are rewarded for helping me.'

Quinn looked at her reproachfully. 'Ah yes, lady, reward me as you would your little dog.'

Elspeth was stung by his words, coming to herself with a jerk. 'No, I did not mean . . .' She saw reproach in his eyes. Impulsively she bent down and took his ugly face between her hands; then, placing her lips full on his, she kissed him. It was the kiss a young woman would give to her lover. She did not draw back as Quinn clasped her to him, returning her gift with a fierce passion. Then he let her go, an oddly sweet smile curving his mouth.

'For that reward I thank you, lady,' he said. 'Go on now.'

Elspeth blinked away her tears, certain that she saw their twin in the dwarf's eyes. 'Thank you,' she whispered. 'God bless you, Quinn. I shall never, never forget you.' Then she was running towards the house.

Quinn watched her go, waiting as she pounded frantically on the imposing front door. He saw it open at last, heard the sound of voices raised in anger; then a tall figure dressed in black appeared in the doorway and Elspeth was drawn inside. Quinn melted into the darkness from whence he came.

Alvar's face was stern as he listened to Elspeth's story. He had hurried her away from the curious eyes of his servants, after barking a series of orders at them which sent them scurrying to prepare the best guest chamber; taking her to a small chamber where the embers of a fire still flickered low in the open hearth. The remains of a meal lay scattered on a table set close to the fire; and it was obvious that Alvar had not long supped. He pulled Elspeth nearer to the flames, throwing another log into the grate and sending a shower of sparks up the chimney. Then he thrust her almost roughly on to the oak settle and pushed a cup of wine into her hands with the command: 'Drink it all!'

Elspeth sipped the wine obediently, her hands trembling as she held the cup to her mouth; but she drained it to the last dregs, handing the empty goblet back to him.

Alvar took it and set it down on the table. Then he knelt before her and took off her shoes; rolling down her wet hose from her knees, he slipped them off too. He began to rub her feet between his hands.

Gradually the wine and Alvar's ministrations relaxed her. She ceased trembling, becoming acutely aware of the intimacy of their situation. She blushed, whispering her thanks.

'Are you warmer now?' he asked, moving away from her. 'My servants will soon have your room ready.'

'I am much better now,' Elspeth replied, hardly daring to look at him. 'I must tell you at once—there is a plot against the King . . .'

Alvar stood up, frowning. 'Who did this to you?' he demanded, his face angry. 'Do you know your sister believes you ran away with a man you met at court? Is that what happened, Elspeth?'

Elspeth stared at him, feeling as though he had struck her. 'Surely Nan cannot have said such a terrible thing! She must know I would not do anything so wicked. I told you just now that I was kidnapped—do you not believe me?'

Alvar's eyes were cold. 'Lady Nanette's message reached me not two hours ago. Your groom said you went willingly—and when the coach did not return . . .'

'I was abducted,' Elspeth cried, her eyes flashing angrily. 'Mr Rathbone offered to take me to Nanette's after I was thrown—but my head hurt so badly and he gave me something which he promised would help relieve the pain. It must have put me to sleep. I have been held prisoner in a house here in London, but tonight I managed to escape . . .'

'So it was Philip Rathbone!' Alvar muttered, a gleam of satisfaction in his eyes. 'You neglected to tell me that at the start, Elspeth. Did you think to protect him? He shall pay for this, I promise you!'

Of course Nanette would never suspect her of running off with a lover! Elspeth suddenly realised she had been tricked into revealing the name of her kidnapper, something she had not meant to do. Her face went white. 'He did not really harm me, Alvar,' she said. 'What you see is the result of an attack upon me by some beggars I chanced to meet. I was saved from worse by Quinn—he is a . . .'

'I know who Quinn is—he is a virtual king of the vagrants in London,' Alvar interrupted her. 'In some areas of the city his word would be obeyed before Henry Tudor's. He shall receive my thanks, never fear. But what if he had not been near when you were set upon by the beggars? Whom should I hold responsible if not Rathbone?'

Elspeth clasped her hands together in her lap. 'He is much to blame—but must you kill him? I am safe enough now.'

Alvar's mouth twisted into a hard sneer. 'Yes, you are

safe enough now.' He laughed bitterly. 'You almost persuade me that you care for Rathbone, Elspeth, and thus seal his fate. Do not waste your breath—he is already dead. Now—you spoke of a plot against the King?'

Elspeth nodded. Looking at the cruel set of Alvar's mouth, she knew there was no use in arguing. He was determined that Philip Rathbone should die for what he had done. She shivered, half afraid of this ruthless man to whom she had given her heart. Philip was doomed, she knew, but she would not give Alvar the name of the man who she believed had helped her to escape—if she did Alvar would probably kill him too!

'I know very little,' she said, avoiding his piercing gaze. 'While I was still barely conscious, Philip and another man came into the room. They thought I was asleep and they spoke about the Earl of Warwick and a boy called—I think they called him Lambert Simnel, but I am not sure. It seemed to be important that I acknowledged this boy as the Earl of Warwick—but I do not know why.'

Alvar nodded. 'We have heard rumours of a plot,' he said. 'It was to discover what I could of their plan that I came to London. I think they mean to set up this Lambert Simnel as the young Earl; then they will rally supporters to his standard and come against Henry.'

Elspeth hesitated, wondering whether she should tell Alvar that the Queen-Dowager's name had been mentioned by the plotters. She decided against it almost at once. She had done her duty: she would not betray a woman who had been kind to her and who might be innocent of any treason. Henry Tudor had an unforgiving nature; if he suspected his wife's mother of plotting against him he would be swift to act—and Elspeth did not wish to harm Elizabeth Woodville.

'I am afraid I have not been of much help to you. I cannot tell you where I was held. After I escaped I just ran blindly into the night.'

Alvar's face softened as he looked at her. 'You have told me all I need to know—and you have proved your loyalty to His Majesty. Henry will be grateful: he cannot deny us the right to marry now. Besides, you will be safer as my wife—safe from those who would seek to use you for their own ends.'

Elspeth trembled as he held out his hand to her. She took it wordlessly, letting him draw her to her feet and into his arms. He seemed to have taken control of her will, and she could only gaze up into his eyes, seeking for a sign of love in him. He said nothing, merely bending his head to take possession of her lips.

He had spoken of their marriage as a foregone conclusion, no longer asking but dictating. As Elspeth surrendered to his kiss, she knew she had never really been free to choose. He meant to have her: he had always meant to possess her—one way or another! She belonged to him. She had been his from the first moment he came to Murran Castle and she looked down at him from the tower. He had sensed it from the beginning, but she had fought against it even after she acknowledged her love for him. Now she could fight no more.

Alvar released her at last, gazing down at her with a mixture of fierce passion, triumph and something else which Elspeth dare not put a name to. 'I had best let you retire to your room, my lady,' he said hoarsely, his breath coming faster, 'or I will not be responsible for my actions. I'll not anticipate our wedding night, Elspeth, though I am sorely tempted.'

Elspeth swayed wearily on her feet. 'I fear you would have scant response, sir. I am so tired I can scarce stand . . .'

Alvar laughed ruefully. 'I am indeed the brute you have so often named me, lady. I talk of love when you have been cruelly used. Forgive me—I thought only of my own need.'

Elspeth smiled at him shyly. For the note of tenderness in his voice she would forgive him anything, she thought.

Alvar lifted her gently in his arms, raising his brow at her smothered protest. 'Come my lady, I will carry you up to your room—and you shall rest safe there. I would have you willing and eager. You shall return to your sister's house while I go on alone to speak with the King, and when I return we shall be wed. Until then you shall remain virgin pure.'

Elspeth sighed, resting her head sleepily against his shoulder. 'I love you,' she whispered, hardly aware that she had spoken.

Alvar's lips brushed against her hair. 'Be still, sweet temptress,' he said, 'the thread that binds your honour is a frail one. Do not press me too far—or it may snap in my hands.'

Elspeth made no reply. He looked down at her and saw that she was already asleep. He smiled wryly, knowing that he might not have been so chivalrous in other circumstances. He strode into the chamber his servants had prepared for her, laying her carefully on the bed. For a moment he stood looking down at her, watching the even flow of her breathing and thinking how innocent she seemed in her sleep. Then he frowned, a picture of another innocent face flashing into his thoughts like a will-o'-the-wisp. He crushed the elusive memory, feeling the pain of it eat into his heart even after so many years. The memory was tainted, long obliterated by others which were like bitter gall in his throat. He forced both the memories and the pain back to the small corner of his mind where they habitually dwelt. He had made his decision, nothing should turn him from it. He bent down to draw a coverlet over Elspeth.

'When you are rested we will go from here,' he said softly, more to himself than to the sleeping girl. Then his face grew hard. 'But first there is something I must do—before we leave the city Philip Rathbone will answer to me for what he dared to do!'

His eyes wore a grim look. Once before he had ridden out into the night in search of revenge. He had taken it ruthlessly, bloodily; but in the aftermath he had walked on the brink of Hell's fiery pit. He still lived in his own private hell; a prison of his own making, from which there was no escape.

Looking down at the sleeping girl, Alvar knew a moment of fear. What right had he to hope for anything from life? Was what he planned a sin so damnable that his soul would rot in Hell for it? His face twisted with pain, his eyes darkening as he considered letting her go even now. He could pretend that the King had refused his permission.

'I cannot,' he whispered, anguish making his voice harsh. 'If I burn in Hell for it, Elspeth, I will have you!'

CHAPTER NINE

It was her wedding day. Elspeth did not know how Alvar had managed to obtain the King's consent to their marriage so swiftly. She would never guess that Henry was glad to dispose of a troublesome debt so easily. She only knew that it was scarcely three weeks since she had fled to Alvar's house in the dark hours of the night. She had had no time to gather bride clothes, and she was to be married in Nanette's wedding gown, which had been altered to fit her slender figure.

She and Nanette were alone now, Nessie having left them while she herself prepared for the wedding. Nanette surveyed the silver brocade gown with a critical eye, sighing.

'You look beautiful, my dear—but it is not fitting that you should be married in such haste. And in an old gown!'

Elspeth laughed, her face alight with an inner beauty which needed neither fine gowns nor jewels to aid it. 'Alvar vows he will not wait, Nan. I must be wed today or he declares he will carry me off without benefit of the priest's blessing. Besides, I like wearing your wedding gown—it is my lucky charm.'

Nanette's smile was slightly anxious. 'You are sure this is what you want, Elspeth? I remember you had doubts before . . .' Nanette's voice faltered as Elspeth's eyes darkened with pain. 'Ah, my dearest sister, forgive me. I should not have mentioned it.'

Elspeth shook her head. 'It is not your fault, Nan. I cannot quite forget the moment when those creatures . . . But I will put it from my mind. I will not think of it—not today.'

Nanette took her hand. 'Nessie said she heard you cry out in your sleep again last night—was it another bad dream?'

Elspeth returned the comforting pressure of her fingers. 'Yes—but do not worry, Nan, I expect they will soon cease to trouble me.' She smiled a little too brightly. 'Do you remember you promised to tell me Alvar's story? You thought it might clear any doubts I still had—will you tell me now, Nan?'

Nanette looked upset. 'I cannot, Elspeth. Alvar has asked that you should not be told—he feels that the old tragedy is best forgotten. He does not want you distressed after what you have recently been through.'

Elspeth felt a cold chill of foreboding—just what was this mystery that lay in Alvar's past? She shrugged her shoulders, pretending an unconcern she did not feel, 'Well, it does not matter. I dare say Alvar will tell me anything I need to know.' She laughed, a sudden surge of joy dispersing her fears. 'Do not be anxious, Nan. I love Alvar. I was meant to be his—I have known it since he first came to the castle. Whatever he is, whatever he has done, I am bound to him. I shall love him until I die.'

Nanette looked relieved. 'Then I have no fears for your happiness, my dear. Love is the most precious gift of all; if you can give it freely, you will reap your own reward.'

'If I am as happy as you are, Nan, I shall be well content.' Elspeth kissed her sister's cheek. 'How is Sir Harold today?'

Nanette's smile deepened. 'Better, I think. He assures me he means to dance at your wedding.' She returned her sister's embrace. 'Yes, I really think he improves at last. He will be glad to see Alvar settled—and with you as his wife. Harold is fond of you, Elspeth.'

'Yes, I know." Elspeth suddenly seized her sister's hands and whirled her round excitedly. 'Wish me joy, Nan! Wish me joy . . .'

* * *

Throughout the wedding ceremony, and the feasting which followed, Elspeth could scarcely take her eyes from Alvar's handsome face. The stern expression he so often wore was gone, and his smile was tender as their eyes met. He looked relaxed, younger than before, as though he had somehow shed a heavy burden he had carried too long. Elspeth felt a pang of love so sharp that it twisted her heart with pain. This was the Alvar she had glimpsed so seldom but had known instinctively.

He had thrown off his bleak mood, discarding it with the sombre black he always wore. Today his tunic was fashioned of a rich blue velvet and trimmed with sable. On his hand he wore a large blue diamond ring; the twin of which was on Elspeth's finger.

Once when she had gazed at his face a little too earnestly, he leaned towards her with a teasing smile. 'And what deep thoughts lie behind that pensive look, my lady?'

Elspeth blushed. Her thoughts had strayed to that moment when all Sir Harold's guests had gone and they would be alone.

'I was thinking that I know so little of you—of your home and family. Will—will they be pleased because you have taken a wife?' she asked, because she was too shy to tell him the truth.

Alvar's eyes darkened as the laughter left them, a spasm of pain passing across his face. 'I have no family but Sir Harold—and you,' he said, his voice taking on that cold note she dreaded. 'My mother died giving birth to a still-born child when I was but a boy. My father never married again, and he himself was killed before I was sixteen. He died fighting for the cause he believed in, and I think he was glad to die. He never ceased to grieve for the wife he had lost—nor to blame himself for her death.'

Elspeth stared at him uncertainly, pity mixing with her love for him. She had never known her mother, but she had had Nanette, her father, step-brothers and Nessie to care for. And, she realised now, with the wisdom only time can bring, it was equally as important to be able to give love as to receive it. For the first time she began to see what had helped to make Alvar the hard, cold man he had seemed when they first met. Instinctively, her hand reached out for his beneath the table, the pressure of her fingers conveying the feelings she could not put into words.

He looked at her thoughtfully. 'I hope you will not find the life too lonely at Alvar, Elspeth. You will have Nessie for company when I am away—but we must find you other companions nearer your own age. Perhaps in time I may be able to arrange for your step-mother and your brothers to visit us—would you like that? I am sorry they could not be here for the wedding, but that the King would not allow.'

Elspeth smiled shyly. 'I shall be happy to see Lady Margaret and my brothers, of course—but I hope you will not be absent too often, my lord?'

Alvar threw back his head and laughed, a teasing light driving the shadows from his eyes. 'Be sure I do not intend to desert my bride too soon. I have served Henry faithfully, and must do so again—but for now the King's cause can wait!'

Elspeth smiled again, her heart pulsing with excitement. Soon now he would take her in his arms and kiss her, and this time there would be no shame in surrendering to the heady joy which surged through her at the touch of his lips. Already she felt weak with the longing to be crushed against his lean, hard body in a passionate embrace; and she could see her own desires reflected and intensified in Alvar's eyes.

As if he could read her mind, Alvar leaned towards her, saying softly, 'The hour grows late, Elspeth, and we have a long journey before us tomorrow. I am sure Sir Harold's guests will forgive you if you retire now. I shall follow you a little later.'

Elspeth nodded, a faint colour rising in her cheeks as

she stood up and moved to Nanette's side, whispering in her ear. Then she left the room, accompanied by her sister and Nessie; and followed by a gentle ripple of laughter and good-natured jests from Sir Harold's elderly friends.

Upstairs in the chamber she was so soon to share with her husband, Elspeth was helped from her stiff silver gown into a softly flowing robe of white silk. Her thick, dark hair was released from its elaborate headdress, and allowed to fall in shining curls on her shoulders.

Nessie wiped away a tear, still unreconciled to the thought of Elspeth as Alvar's bride, though Elspeth had assured her many times of her willingness to wed him.

'You look like an angel,' she sniffed, shuddering inwardly as she imagined Elspeth in the arms of 'that man' as she still thought of Alvar. 'An innocent babe . . .'

Nanette gave her a disapproving look. 'We will have none of that nonsense, Nessie,' she said, in a tone which was severe for her. 'Elspeth is not a child, and she has chosen freely. She is going to be just as happy as she deserves.'

Elspeth kissed her sister, then held out her hands to Nessie. 'Wish me joy, Nessie. I promise you this is what I want.'

Nessie sniffed again, then drew Elspeth into a fervent hug. 'Well, as long as you are sure . . .' she broke off as Alvar came into the room.

'Forgive me,' he said, his eyes seeking Elspeth's briefly, and then turning to Nanette. 'I bring bad news—Sir Harold was taken suddenly ill after you left. We carried him to his chamber . . .'

Nanette gave a little cry, her face going white. 'Oh no! He isn't . . .' She clutched at Alvar's arm desperately. 'Tell me he is not dead!'

Alvar looked at her with pity, his voice gentle as he said: 'I think not, Lady Nanette, but he is very weak and asking for you.'

'I must go to him.'

Nanette ran from the room, and Elspeth started after her. Then she halted and turned to look at Alvar, a desperate appeal for understanding in her eyes. 'I must go with her,' she said, her voice catching. 'She needs me.'

'Of course you must go to her,' Alvar said. 'There will be other nights for us—but first put a wrap over your night-rail. I would not have you take a chill.'

'Here, put this on, my lady,' Nessie said, bringing a robe of crimson velvet with long, full sleeves for Elspeth to slip on over her silken nightgown.

Elspeth thanked her absently, her anxiety making her anxious to follow Nanette. Giving Alvar a brief smile of apology, she ran swiftly down the passage to the sick man's bedchamber, joining her sister beside his bed.

In the dim light of the candle, Sir Harold's face was a ghastly shade of ivory as he struggled for life. The sound of his ragged breathing filled the room, and it was terrible to hear. Elspeth's fingers entwined with Nan's, gripping them tightly.

'You should not be here,' Nanette whispered, but her voice shook and she clasped her sister's hand gratefully. 'Your place is with your husband.'

Elspeth shook her head. 'Alvar understands—my place is with you tonight.'

Nanette knew that she ought to send Elspeth away, but for once her strength of mind deserted her. She desperately needed the reassurance of her sister's company.

'Oh, Elspeth,' she said, her voice breaking on a sob. 'I am so afraid he is going to die—and he is such a dear, good man.'

Looking at Sir Harold's tortured face, Elspeth could find no words for comfort. He seemed close to death, as though his soul was all but ready to quit his pain-racked body. Putting her arms about Nanette, she drew her close, offering her love instead of useless sympathy.

'All we can do is pray, my dearest,' she said, her eyes flickering above Nan's head to Alvar who had come quietly into the room. 'All we can do is pray . . .'

As the night wore on Sir Harold's breathing eased a little, and the sickly, yellow tones began to fade from his cheeks. Soon after dawn the physician pronounced the crisis over for the moment, saying that he thought Sir Harold now stood a chance of recovery, though it would be slow and he would be confined to his bed for a long time. It seemed that Sir Harold had escaped the Reaper's scythe this time.

Nanette turned to Elspeth, feeling calmer now. 'You must get some rest, my dear. You have helped me more than you know, but I shall manage now—and you have a long journey before you.'

'But we cannot leave—not while Sir Harold is so ill!'

Nanette smiled at her. 'You must go, my love. You have your own life to live, your own home waiting for you. I would not have it otherwise. You were here when I needed you—you must think of yourself and Alvar. Besides, it would worry Harold to know you tarried here for his sake. I will send you word when I can.'

Elspeth sent a look of appeal to her husband. 'Tell her, my lord—tell her we will not leave.'

Alvar shrugged his broad shoulders. 'We will stay if Lady Nanette desires it, Elspeth, but I think she is right. We would only be an added burden on her household at this time.'

Elspeth stared at him in dismay. She had not given a thought to the extra work feeding Alvar and his men must mean for Nanette's servants. Glancing at her sister's face she saw that it was true, though Nanette would not say so.

'I had not thought . . .' she faltered. 'But I cannot bear that you should be alone at such a time—I will leave Nessie with you, Nan. You may need her to help your nurse Sir Harold, and it will be a comfort for you to have her to talk with when you are anxious.'

Nanette was about to protest, but the words died unspoken on her lips. Nessie could not hide her dislike of Elspeth's marriage; it might be better for them both if she remained behind, at least for a while.

'Thank you, my dear. I confess it would be a comfort to have Nessie with me.' Lady Nanette smiled at her sister. 'I will send one of my maids with you—perhaps Mally. Yes, Mally is a sensible girl, she shall go with you. But now you really must get some rest. I shall sit here a little longer.'

Elspeth nodded. Glancing once more at Sir Harold, who seemed to have passed into a restful sleep, she bent and kissed Nan's cheek; then she gave her hand to Alvar with a smile. 'Very well, we will leave now. God keep you, my dearest—and Sir Harold.'

'Bless you, my love—go now.'

Elspeth smiled, allowing Alvar to draw her from the room. Once outside she leaned her head against his chest, giving way to tears. 'My poor, poor Nan,' she said, drawing back and looking up at him. 'Do you think Sir Harold will recover?'

Alvar's face was grave. 'This time, perhaps, but the end cannot be long. I think Lady Nanette knows it. She was shocked tonight because he had seemed so much better these past few days—but I am sure she has been prepared for it for some while.'

Elspeth sighed, smothering a yawn. 'I know, she is so brave . . .'

Alvar looked down at her, a half-smile quirking the corners of his mouth. 'And you are weary, my lady.' Bending down he lifted her in his arms.

Smiling up at him, Elspeth nestled against his shoulder as he strode down the passage to their room. She murmured a faint protest as he laid her on the bed, missing the warmth of his body and trying vainly not to close her eyes. She felt the touch of his lips against her hair, then his voice whispering in her ear:

'Sleep now, my darling, it seems I must be patient a little longer . . .'

Elspeth glanced sideways at her husband's face. They had been riding for most of the day now, and she was tired; but he showed no sign of strain, though he had not slept all the previous night. After leaving her to rest, he had directed the preparations for their journey, waking her only when they were almost ready to leave. She had dressed hastily, having no time to do more than kiss Nanette goodbye and reassure herself that Sir Harold was no worse. Alvar had deliberately planned it so, she realised, understanding that a lengthy farewell would lead to tears.

Nessie had not at first believed that she was to be left behind; but Nanette calmed her angry indignation by begging her to stay for her sake. Obviously torn between the two sisters, Nessie gave in at last, believing that Nanette needed her more; though her reluctance to part with Elspeth showed in her face, and she bewildered poor Mally with a hundred last minute instructions on the care of Lady Alvar's clothes.

Hearing the faint sigh which escaped Elspeth's lips, Alvar studied her face. 'Soon we shall reach a shallow ford in the river. We will rest there and refresh ourselves while the horses quench their thirst. I know you are tired, Elspeth, but I want to reach Alvar Manor tonight—there are no respectable inns where we could stay, and it is not so very much further.

Elspeth nodded. It was some hours since they had passed a village; and the countryside through which they rode was becoming increasingly more lonely and wild. For the last several miles they had been following a fast-flowing river through a deep valley, hemmed in on either side by steep hills covered in prickly furze bushes. The hills seemed almost impenetrable, the passes too dangerous for any living thing to negotiate, except, perhaps, a mountain goat or an eagle nesting in the craggy upper reaches.

Overhead the dark shadow of a buzzard glided and circled, its mewing cry echoing eerily in the stillness as the song birds hushed, fearing death from the sky. A sudden swoop and a small, furry creature struggled helplessly in cruel talons as the broad, moth-like wings beat a leisurely retreat. Elspeth shivered, reminded of something which had lain dormant in her memory for a long time.

Her eyes rested briefly on the back of one of Alvar's men, recognising the square set of his shoulders. She recalled her last meeting with Firkin, when she had vowed to be revenged on Alvar one day. How far away that day seemed now, and how foolish the girl who had struggled against her destiny! She turned to Alvar, smiling, her dark eyes glowing with love.

'Do not worry about me,' she said, lifting her head proudly. 'I am as eager to reach Alvar Manor tonight as you are.'

Alvar's mouth curved in a smile of approval, but he made no reply, merely nodding before spurring his horse forward to speak with one of his men.

The light was fast fading as they neared the lands Alvar's ancestors had held since William of Normandy first vanquished the Saxon King Harold at Hastings. The steep hills had given way to bleak heathland, bare of its summer dress of purple heather; and then, at last, to treacherous salt marshes and the tang of the sea. They passed through a small village clustered about the mouth of the tributary, where the river they had followed spilled out in a frenzy, flowing eventually to the sea.

Then Elspeth saw the house which was to be her home. Half fortress, half manor house, it stood against a backdrop of sheer cliffs; not built into the granite as Murran Castle was, but on a wide plateau overlooking the bay and the surrounding countryside. Alvar's ancestors had chosen well, she saw, for an enemy must pass the village when approaching the fortress, whether they came from the land or the sea. The cliffs were too sheer to climb, and the only other way led through treacherous marshes with secret paths known only to the local people. A surprise attack would be virtually impossible, and the stout walls looked as though they could withstand the most determined assault.

The house had no moat, but a portcullis guarded the main gate, and it had two huge towers at either side, pierced with arrow loops from which an archer could wreak havoc on the attacking force below. Once through the gate, Elspeth saw that parts of the house were much newer than others and had obviously been rebuilt in the last few years.

Alvar's eyes followed her curious gaze. 'There was a fire,' he said, a tense muscle pulsing in his neck. 'Part of the original fortress was gutted—so I had it rebuilt.'

Elspeth's attention was drawn to a stone tower right on the edge of the cliffs. 'That must be part of the old fortress,' she said. 'It seems to be almost separate from the rest of the house.'

'It is connected by a passage—but no one goes there these days. It is unsafe since the fire.' He slipped to the ground, giving the reins to a groom who had come running. Then he held out his arms to Elspeth, swinging her down to the ground and looking into her eyes for a moment. 'Welcome to Alvar, my lady . . .'

An elderly servant hovered anxiously at Alvar's elbow. 'We had no word you were coming, my lord,' he said, eyeing Elspeth with unspoken curiosity. 'You find us sadly unprepared.'

Alvar frowned. 'I sent word three days ago—did my messenger not arrive?'

The servant swallowed nervously. 'A messenger came, my lord, but we were given no instructions.'

Alvar's mouth drew into a tight line, a cold light in his blue eyes. 'I did not think she would dare to disobey me, but I should have known she is an insolent bitch who would dare anything!' He turned to Elspeth, taking her arm and drawing her forward. 'Osric, this is Lady Elspeth—my new bride. I want you to see that my mother's chamber is prepared for her use.'

Osric's mouth fell open, but Elspeth did not see the startled look in his eyes. Alvar had hurried her on into the house. They were standing in the main hall, and at their right was a wooden stairway leading to a gallery above.

'Your—wife, my lord?' Osric questioned foolishly.

Alvar's face hardened and his voice seemed to carry a note of warning as he repeated, 'My wife, Osric, your new mistress. Well, is this the way you welcome your lord's wife? Where are your wits, man?'

Osric swallowed hard, bowing awkwardly to Elspeth. 'Your pardon, my lady. I am steward to Lord Alvar, and I bid you welcome most willingly. I beg you will forgive my boorish manners, but we did not know. Myfanwy said nothing . . .' He broke off in confusion as Alvar made a furious sound in his throat. 'Pardon, my lord, I did not mean . . .'

'Oh, be silent, you dithering fool!' Alvar exclaimed, glaring at him.

Elspeth stared at her husband, bewildered by his sudden change of mood. Yet it was not really so sudden, for she had noticed he grew more thoughtful as they neared his home, and she had guessed his thoughts were not all pleasant by the bleak expression in his eyes. She shivered, wondering at this new change of mood—why had her tender lover become a hard stranger once more?

'Who is Myfanwy?' she asked innocently. 'It is a name I have not heard before.'

Alvar frowned, his face set hard as though he did not want to answer her question. 'Myfanwy is . . .' he said, breaking off as a low, musical voice interrupted him.

'I am Myfanwy, my lady.'

Elspeth turned to look in the direction from whence

the voice came. A woman paused at the head of the stairs, her red hair gleaming in the flare of the torch she carried, its flames highlighting her beautiful face. She began to walk towards them, her body swaying with the slow, sensual rhythm of a cat. She halted a few feet from Elspeth, an insolent smile playing about her full mouth.

'I bid you welcome to Alvar Manor, my lady.'

The soft voice stroked like a velvet glove, but Elspeth instinctively distrusted its owner. Gazing into the other woman's green eyes, she felt a band of ice tightening about her heart. 'Who are you?' she asked, her voice a harsh whisper. 'What is your position here?'

Myfanwy's eyes glittered with malice. She glanced at Alvar mockingly. 'Shall I tell her?' she asked, her body shaking with silent laughter as she saw the unmistakable start of fear in his face. Then she murmured something in a language which Elspeth could not understand; but her words brought first anger and then relief to Alvar's eyes. He replied in the same tongue sharply, and Myfanwy's face became sullen.

Elspeth felt a spurt of anger. They were deliberately using this strange language so that she could not understand what they said. She tilted her head proudly, her body taut with anger.

'Well—is someone going to tell me who she is?' she demanded.

Alvar hesitated and the woman's face lost its sullen look, a gloating expression creeping into her eyes as she silently dared him to speak the truth.

'She is a distant cousin—she has acted as my housekeeper for some years, that is all,' he said at last, and Elspeth knew he was lying.

CHAPTER TEN

ELSPETH stared at Alvar's face, the band of ice tightening about her heart as she read the guilt written there. In that moment she knew that this beautiful, insolent woman was far more to her husband than a distant relation who acted as his housekeeper. It was obvious she enjoyed a privileged position in his household, and that she had been on intimate terms with him. She had been his mistress, probably for several years before he left the manor. That she still had considerable influence with him was apparent in the bold way she had chosen to confront them, almost as though she was determined to flaunt her existence before Elspeth's eyes, and believed herself powerful enough to escape retribution.

Elspeth waited in silence, hoping that Alvar would say something which would prove her suspicions wrong. She felt she could bear anything if only he would send this beautiful, sensuous woman out of her sight. She waited as the tension stretched between them until it was as taut as a bowstring before the arrow flies. Alvar seemed to be suspended in some private hell of his own, incapable of speech, his eyes mirroring his inner torment.

Elspeth lifted her head proudly, her eyes flashing with anger. 'I am tired,' she said, her lips stiff with the effort to speak calmly. She would not give way to her feelings in front of Myfanwy. She would not give her the satisfaction of seeing how much pain she had inflicted. 'I should like to go to my room.'

'Of course, my lady.' Myfanwy curtsied mockingly. 'I have prepared your chamber with my own hands. I will take you there if you will follow me.'

Alvar suddenly seemed to snap back to life, his mouth hardening into a thin line . . . 'Which room have you prepared for my wife?' he asked, his voice grating harshly, an underlying violence scraping the surface and bringing a flash of fear to Myfanwy's eyes for the first time.

'Why, the chamber which was your mother's, my lord.' Realising that she had pushed him too far, Myfanwy's voice became deceptively humble. 'I have obeyed your orders in this—as always.' A gleam of sly malice flashed from the slitted green eyes.

Alvar's features might have been carved from granite as he stared at her. He was once more in possession of his emotions, only the white knuckles of the hand resting on his sword hilt betrayed his rage.

Looking at him, Elspeth wondered if she had imagined the start of fear she had seen in his eyes when Myfanwy first confronted them. But no, it had been there, she was sure. What hold had this woman over Alvar that she could flaunt herself before him and still escape the lash of his tongue?

Elspeth's thoughts were scattered as he turned to her, holding out his hand imperiously. 'Come, Elspeth, I shall take you to your chamber myself.'

'Thank you, my lord,' Elspeth replied coolly, ignoring his outstretched hand.

For a few seconds their eyes met, and Elspeth seemed to read an appeal for understanding in Alvar's steady, blue gaze. Fleetingly she glimpsed a depth of suffering which was beyond her comprehension, shaking her out of her mood of self-righteous indignation. But even as she wondered what could have brought that tormented look to her husband's eyes, he had turned away and she was left to follow him as best she could as he strode past Myfanwy and on up the stairs.

As Elspeth drew level with the other woman she seemed as though she would bar the way. They stared at one another, each testing the other's will, and it was Myfanwy who turned away. Tossing her head angrily, she vented her fury on the servants who had silently gathered in the hall to witness the little scene. As Myfanwy moved out of Elspeth's way, there was a low sighing sound as though of relief.

Continuing up the stairs, Elspeth could hear Myfanwy berating the luckless servants, and the peevish tone of the older woman's voice was as music to her ears. Somehow she knew she had won the first skirmish, but the battle was far from over. Myfanwy would not easily relinquish her position in Alvar's household, that much was clear.

Elspeth felt a renewed surge of anger as she pondered just what that position might be. Jealousy flared in her like a torch. Surely Alvar did not expect his wife and his former mistress to live side by side in the same household! No matter how vast the house was, they were bound to meet sometimes. It was humiliating. Alvar had no right to bring her here in such circumstances, common decency demanded that he send his mistress away immediately.

Alvar was striding ahead of her so that she was forced to quicken her pace to keep up with him for fear of becoming lost in the bewildering maze of passages. A sudden, sharp turn to the left brought them to a short flight of stairs. Pausing briefly to glance through the window at the foot of the steps, Elspeth saw a small, inner courtyard, tiled and enclosed with flowering shrubs. She just had time to reflect how pleasant it would be to stroll there on a spring day when Alvar called to her impatiently from the top of the stairs.

She looked up to see him holding a door open for her. 'These rooms once belonged to my mother,' he said as she joined him, an odd, defensive note in his voice. 'No one has used them since she died. My father wanted them kept just as she left them, and I have respected his wishes—until now. I hope you will find them comfortable. You must make whatever changes you wish, of course.'

Elspeth winced at the chill politeness in his voice, but allowed no sign of her feelings to show as she followed him into the first room.

Candles had been lit only a short time earlier, and a small fire was burning in the grate. It was obvious that some efforts had been made to clean the rooms; and Alvar gave an audible sigh of relief, as though he had feared to find them hung with cobwebs and the dust of years.

Elspeth let her eyes travel slowly round the room, noting the stone floor freshly strewn with aromatic herbs, and the oak-panelled walls. The furniture consisted of a carved cupboard, a heavy oak table with bulbous supports and a small chair with x-shaped scroll legs; all of which looked dull as though they had not been waxed for years. On the table lay a leather-bound bible with a silver clasp, together with a weighty silver candlestick. Above the fireplace hung a faded tapestry depicting the crucifixion, and a large, wooden cross adorned another wall.

Alvar's mother had been a devout lady, Elspeth thought as she passed on into the bedchamber and saw another crucifix above the large four-poster bed.

Alvar frowned as he followed Elspeth's gaze. 'I gave orders that my mother's personal belongings were to be removed. I shall send a servant to take all these things away.'

'No!' Elspeth exclaimed involuntarily, blushing at his raised brows. 'Leave them—they belong here. They do not displease me.'

Alvar shrugged, his lips twisting cynically. 'As you wish.' He inspected the bed hangings with a critical eye, frowning as he saw they had begun to rot with age and disuse. 'These will have to be changed—but at least the linen is fresh, that much has been done. I will not try to apologise for the sorry welcome you have been offered in my house, Elspeth. It is a long time since I was here—I see that I have not returned a moment too soon.'

Elspeth stared at him uncertainly. He had once more become the coldly polite stranger who had escorted her to King Henry's court under armed guard. Anger flared in her swiftly. How dare he retreat behind that barrier of indifference? She was his wife. She would not be treated as though she were some casual guest of little importance!

'Who is that woman that she dare flout your orders?' she demanded, anger loosening her tongue now that they were alone.

'I told you, she has helped to keep my house for me since—since these past nine years.'

'Do not lie to me, sir!' Elspeth ignored the warning signs in his face, driven on by a fury equal to any which might be simmering beneath his mask of indifference. 'I think she has been much more to you. Can you deny it? Can you deny she has been your mistress?'

Elspeth looked into his eyes, her heart contracting with pain as she saw her answer reflected there. For a moment as he hesitated she thought he would try to lie to her again, then he shrugged his shoulders, sighing.

'I thought it might be easier for you if you did not know. I suppose I should have realised that you would guess the truth—but I had not bargained for that little scene earlier. I ought to have warned you. I am sorry, Elspeth, can you forgive me?'

Once again Elspeth thought she saw a deep sadness in his eyes, but she resolutely steeled her heart against him. What right had he to look at her like that when it was she who had been wronged?

'I shall find it hard to do so, my lord, while that woman remains beneath your roof. I demand that you send her away immediately.'

Alvar frowned. 'If that were possible, do you not think it would already have been done?'

Elspeth stared at him in disbelief. 'What do you

mean? Are you saying you will not send her away?'

Alvar's face hardened. 'I am saying I cannot send her away. She is needed here.'

Elspeth gasped, feeling as though he had struck her. 'Do you intend to . . .' she was unable to continue, turning away as the sickness caught at her throat.

Alvar's hands were less than gentle as he swung her back to face him. 'No, I do not intend to bed with her,' he said, anger in his voice now. He dragged her towards a small door at the rear of her bedchamber which she had not noticed before, opening it and thrusting her roughly into the next room. 'This is where I shall sleep, unless I choose to stay in my wife's bed, that is. This was my father's room—and no, she has never been here. Anything that was between us is over, Elspeth, I swear it.'

Elspeth looked at him, desperately wanting to believe him. 'Then—why won't you send her away?'

'Because I cannot!' Alvar's face was taut with strain. 'By God! Have I wed a shrew? Must I beg for forgiveness on my knees? If that's what you want, madam, you ask too much. Did you expect me to have lived like a monk all my life?'

'No . . .' Elspeth's voice was barely a whisper. 'No, I did not expect that.'

'Then what?' Alvar's eyes searched her white face, seeing the lingering doubts. 'Are you asking for my promise that I will never lie with her again? You have it—I swear it by all I hold sacred.'

'And yet you will not send her away.' Elspeth set her chin at him stubbornly. 'Why did you wed me, my lord? You were not so inclined to it until Lady Ursula left me her fortune. You must think me a fool to be duped so easily. You never spoke of love, and yet I believed you cared for me . . .' Elspeth's voice broke on a sob and she tried to brush past him, but he caught her in his arms and held her tight.

She struggled fiercely, hating him for bringing her close to shameful tears. He tipped her head back, forcing her to look up into his face and her struggles ceased as she saw the bleak expression in his eyes, her blood running cold.

'What is love, Elspeth?' he asked, his soft voice made harsh by the grating pain inside him. 'Once I thought I knew—but all that I loved died a long time ago, and I am no longer sure of anything. If loving means that I would risk my soul's eternal damnation to have you as my wife, then I do most surely love you.'

Something in his voice hushed the protest on her lips so that she could not ask him what he meant. She sensed that she was dangerously close to discovering a secret which might destroy them both, and she was suddenly afraid. She was silent, passive, as he drew her closer, his face full of a desperate hunger.

'Is this love, Elspeth?' he asked hoarsely, his hand shaking as he touched her dark tresses. 'Or is it the Devil's work? Are you here in my arms at last—or will you vanish when I reach for you as you do in my dreams?'

Elspeth could not answer him. That Alvar felt some strong emotion for her she could no longer doubt. He was like a man in torment, trembling from head to foot. She made no resistance as he gathered her up in his arms and carried her to his bed.

His fingers were clumsy in their haste as he tore at the fastenings of her gown; but now the urgency of his need had communicated itself to her and she was on fire with an impatience which matched Alvar's own, forgetting her anger as she returned his feverish kisses.

'Let me help you, my lord,' she whispered, easing up her hips so he could free her of her hampering petticoats.

Now she lay naked in his arms. Alvar looked at her, drinking in the beauty of her creamy-white flesh as though his thirst for her could never be slaked. 'You are so lovely,' he breathed, his hand caressing her breast almost reverently. 'Far too lovely to be real. I think I have conjured you up from my dreams . . .'

Elspeth closed her eyes, hot tears building behind the lids. It was as though she moved in a dream; even when she felt the cool hardness of his flesh against hers, she scarcely knew what was happening to her. It was a fevered dream; a dream in which the man who took possession of her body was as much a slave of the tortured passion which drove him as she. She cried out at the sharp, tearing pain as he entered her, but he seemed beyond all reasoning, deaf to her soft whimpering as she moved beneath him. But then the pain was forgotten as she was swept up into the feverish fantasy once more, and her moans were cries of pleasure. She writhed uncontrollably, panting, dizzy with a reeling ecstasy.

Then it was over, and she lay beside him as he rolled away from her, drained of all emotion, as though he had torn her very soul from her body. She became aware that he was bending over her. His fingers traced her cheeks, wiping away the tears she had not known she shed. He lifted her hand, turning it to kiss the palm with a curious gentleness.

'I am sorry if I hurt you, Elspeth,' he said, his voice soft and caressing now. 'I did not mean it to be like that—forgive me. I have wanted you too much for too long.'

Elspeth turned her head on the pillow to look at him. 'You did not hurt me, my lord,' she whispered. 'At least—only a little.'

Alvar touched her hair. 'I will be gentle with you next time,' he promised, a rueful expression in his eyes. 'I was afraid that if I did not have you now I should lose you. Now you are mine; you cannot leave me.'

Elspeth wrinkled her brow, puzzled. 'How could I leave you, my lord? I am your wife.'

For a brief moment the bleak look was back in Alvar's eyes, then he smiled and bent to brush his lips against hers. 'Yes, you are my wife,' he said, a savage triumph in his voice. 'Mine. My wife. My own. I would kill anyone who sought to take you from me—as I killed Philip Rathbone.'

Elspeth trembled, sitting up with a jerk of horror. 'I hoped you would forget what he had done. Was it really necessary to murder him?'

A hard light glowed in Alvar's eyes. 'Murder, Elspeth? It was a fair match, I promise you. Rathbone was a skilled swordsman. Better he should die by the sword than hang as a traitor.'

Elspeth shivered. 'I suppose so,' she said, 'but revenge is bitter gall. I once saw a score of men die at my order and I found no pleasure in it, though they were murderers and deserved their fate.'

Alvar frowned, an odd, distant look in his eyes turning them to blue ice. 'What do you know of revenge—or the torment of utter despair?' he asked, his voice hard. 'You were but a child when your men killed those raiders—oh, yes, I know what happened, there is nothing I do not know of you—and they had harmed none of your kin. Imagine what you might have felt if they had destroyed someone you loved . . .'

Elspeth stared at him, suddenly sure that she was about to discover something important. 'Is that—is that why you killed the Baron all those years ago?'

Alvar moved his head slightly in assent, then he slid from the bed and began to dress in the clothes he had abandoned earlier.

His face was turned away from her as he said: 'I was betrothed to someone once. Baron Cassell stole her from me—so I killed him.'

Elspeth smothered a gasp. So this was what Nanette had wanted to tell her! 'And—what happened to your betrothed?' she asked, trembling as she waited for his answer.

'She died.' Alvar turned to face her, and she was shocked at the naked pain in his eyes. 'All that I loved in her died, and the man I had been died too. Do not blame me for what I am, Elspeth, blame a god who has no justice. Blame the Devil who spawned an evil creature like the Baron—but do not hate me; for if you do, you cast me back into the hell I have struggled to escape for your sake.'

Elspeth felt the shock of his words run through her, experiencing a little of his pain. 'I do not think I could ever hate you, my lord.'

Alvar smiled oddly. 'Even if you did I do not believe I could let you go now. I have you—as I promised the first time we met. Do you remember?'

Elspeth moved slightly, her dark hair falling like a curtain over her breasts. 'Could I ever forget? Why did you speak so to me, my lord? I have often wondered . . .'

Alvar looked surprised. 'Do you really not know? It was because my pride was hurt. I had thought your father must have told you—I asked him for your hand in marriage and he refused. I believed it was because you had shown your dislike of such a match—was it not so?'

Elspeth shook with helpless laughter. She struggled to control her amusement as she saw Alvar's bewilderment. 'Oh, my lord, forgive me for my mirth. Did you really believe the Earl of Murran would heed the wishes of a mere female? If he refused your offer—then he had reasons of his own.'

Alvar returned to the bed and sat down beside her. 'Then I wronged you, Elspeth. It was because I believed you had scorned me that I treated you so coldly when we next met. I had had well over a year to brood upon it, remember—and then I heard you plotting with Firkin to kill me . . .'

Elspeth felt the colour rush to her cheeks. 'I almost hated you then,' she whispered. 'You were my enemy—and you brought the news of my father's death.'

'A sorry beginning.' Alvar traced the curve of her neck with his fingertips. 'Will you believe me now when I say I want only to make you happy? Will you trust me,

Elspeth—in all things? Even those you do not understand?'

Elspeth felt her blood pulse in her veins, desire churning in her at his touch. How could she refuse? How could she say she did not trust him when her whole body clamoured insistently for his? She deliberately shut the memory of Myfanwy's bold, insolent face out of her mind, realising that she must learn to live with the knowledge that the other woman had once been Alvar's mistress, had thrilled to his caress even as she was doing now.

She raised her eyes and looked into his. 'I will trust you, my lord,' she said, 'until you give me cause to do otherwise.'

Alvar laughed suddenly, a hard gleam in his eyes. 'And then you would sink your fangs into my throat, my little she-wolf, wouldn't you? Oh, do not trouble to deny it—your fierce pride is part of all I prize in you. I knew from the start that you were a fit mate for the Wolf of Alvar. I believe even I would find it hard to crush your spirit.'

He leant towards her, brushing his lips lightly against hers. He smiled as he felt her instant response, drawing back as she would have melted into his arms.

'Not yet, my darling,' he murmured, laughing softly. 'I have treated you ill enough for one night. We have travelled far this day—and I did not give you time to so much as change your gown. I can hear your maid hovering on the other side of that door. I will let her come to you now. Later I shall return for you and we will sup together.'

Alvar stood up, and Elspeth keened the loss of him, wanting to keep him near her. 'Where are you going?' she asked.

Alvar frowned. 'I have been absent too long,' he said, harsh lines about his mouth. 'It seems that there are those who must learn my orders are to be obeyed.'

Elspeth shivered. In that moment she could almost

feel sorry for Myfanwy. 'You are going to her?' she asked, a note of accusation creeping into her voice though she fought to suppress it.

'Doubting me already?' Alvar sighed. 'I promise you have no need to, Elspeth. Surely you cannot believe I would go from your bed to hers?'

Elspeth shook her head, feeling ashamed of the jealousy which twisted and clawed inside her. 'No—I do not think that, my lord.' She looked at him like a bewildered child. 'But why must she stay here?'

'If I told you that you might hate me,' Alvar said, the deep sadness in his eyes once more. 'Believe that I do what I must, Elspeth. Do not ask me that which would destroy us both.'

Elspeth was silent as he left the room, staring after him in dismay. Alvar asked for her trust, and she wanted to give him all that he asked, but something inside her would not let her surrender to him completely. They had talked a great deal tonight, coming closer to understanding each other than ever before. Yet she knew that Alvar still held something back from her—something so terrible that he dare not speak of it!

It was because of this secret that Myfanwy had dared to confront them so boldly. She knew what Elspeth did not, and because of her knowledge Alvar was afraid to send her away.

Alvar, who feared no man, feared to tell Elspeth the truth. What was this terrible secret which lay in his past? Elspeth knew that they would never be truly happy while the mystery hung between them, there would always be doubts and small lies to shroud the truth. Yet she was afraid to probe too hard, for fear that the fragile bonds which bound Alvar to her might somehow snap.

'Trust me,' Alvar had said.

What else could she do? She was his wife, and he would never let her go!

CHAPTER ELEVEN

ELSPETH stirred into wakefulness, her hand moving across the bed of its own volition, seeking the warmth of Alvar's body. Finding the sheets cold to the touch, she sighed, stretching voluptuously in the luxury of the soft bed, a little smile curving her lips as memories of the previous night came trickling into her mind like sunbeams dancing on water. She could still feel the imprint of Alvar's kisses on her mouth, and her flesh still tingled with the sensuous pleasure his passionate love-making evoked from her.

They had been at Alvar Manor for nearly three weeks now, and during that time Elspeth had learned to welcome the hours she spent in her husband's arms each night. In the curtained privacy of their bed, he had taught her the delights of physical love, bringing her to a new awareness of her own body. For after that first time, which had been little short of brutal, Alvar had been a gentle, tender lover. Never since that night had he let his own need overcome concern for her pleasure, and sometimes Elspeth truly believed their first loving had been the fevered dream it seemed.

'Will you rise now, my lady?'

With some reluctance, Elspeth brought her wandering thoughts back to the present moment, smiling at her maid as Mally drew the heavy curtains aside. Alvar's love-making was almost like a drug, leaving her sleepily content and unwilling to rise in the mornings.

'Yes, I suppose so, Mally.' Elspeth laughed happily. 'I am become a sluggard. If Nessie were here she would scold me for wasting half the day abed.'

Mally gave her a knowing look. 'Lord Alvar said I was to let you sleep on, my lady.'

Elspeth smiled. It was no use being shy with Mally; she had seen the bruises on her mistress's flesh left by Alvar's first brutal possession. And she knew that Elspeth had not once slept alone since that night.

'Where is my lord?' Elspeth asked, getting out of bed and slipping on the wrap Mally held ready for her. She sat down so that Mally could brush her long hair and braid it high into two coils on either side of her head.

'I believe he went out with some of his men, my lady. Osric has been training a young kestrel for him and he wanted to put it to the test.'

Elspeth nodded. 'Yes, I remember he spoke of it yesterday.' She stretched lazily and yawned. 'If he had woken me I would have gone with him—I used to accompany my father sometimes.'

'Perhaps my lord thought you needed to rest,' Mally said, giving her a sly look before turning away to the huge armoire in the corner of the room. 'Which gown will you wear today, my lady—the blue or the green?'

'I shall wear the blue velvet with my girdle of silver threads,' Elspeth replied, standing up so that Mally could lower the gown over her head. It clung to her slender waist, emphasising her high, firm breasts and swirling about her hips to brush the floor with a short train. Mally fastened the girdle around her waist, then brought a fur-trimmed mantle for her to wear over her gown.

Elspeth glanced at herself in the small Venetian mirror Alvar had given her as a wedding gift. It was finely wrought in silver and gilt, and Elspeth prized it above all her trinkets. Her father had condemned such vanities as frivolous, but Alvar had given her many lovely presents; chains of gold entwined with rare stones he had brought back from his travels abroad, pearls, laces, silks and precious perfumes.

'You grow more lovely every day, my lady,' Mally

said. 'I do think marriage favours you.'

Elspeth laughed. 'Be quiet, you wretched girl! I have borne enough of your slyness this morning. I shall go down and walk in the courtyard.'

Mally grinned. 'Yes, my lady. The breeze is cool, but the air will do you good.'

Elspeth ignored the girl's parting shot, knowing that she preferred Mally's teasing to the dour looks she would have had from Nessie. Nessie would have exclaimed over the dark bruises on Elspeth's flesh, and condemned Alvar as a thoughtless brute. She could never have understood that Elspeth wore those bruises as a badge of pride, glorying in the knowledge of the desperate passion she had roused in her husband. If she had once believed he wed her for the sake of Aunt Ursula's fortune, she had ceased to believe it now. He had showered her with expensive gifts. Nor could she doubt that he drew as much pleasure as she from their love-filled nights.

Elspeth passed one of Alvar's servants on the staircase leading down to the little inner courtyard. He stood aside respectfully to let her pass, acknowledging her with a bow of his head. Elspeth smiled slightly. She had never known what took place that first night after Alvar left her, but from that time on his servants had been quick to show her the respect due to their lord's wife.

Her orders were obeyed with an alacrity which spoke volumes of the awe in which Alvar was held by his minions; though she seldom gave an order, for the household needed no direction from its new mistress. Fresh drapes had appeared for her bed the next morning; and all the little things which helped to make her chamber comfortable soon followed, transforming the rather austere atmosphere of the room. Elspeth was enchanted with her new home, finding it far more pleasant than the cold, draughty castle in which she had been raised.

For the most part she was happy, and the few doubts

she had came from the strange moods which gripped her husband from time to time. One moment he would be her teasing, tender lover, the next she would turn to find him watching her with an odd expression in his eyes. If she asked him what was wrong, he shook his head, pretending all was well; and sometimes he would go off alone for several hours, returning with that bleak look she dreaded in his eyes.

So far she had not come face to face with Myfanwy since that first night, though she had glimpsed her passing through the hall once. Elspeth believed her husband had warned Myfanwy to keep away from her. And though they often dined in the hall with Alvar's men and the other members of the household, Myfanwy was never there.

As yet Elspeth had not been able to accept the fact that Alvar's former mistress was still living in the house. It was the one thorn in her flesh, the one threat to her happiness. And try as she might, she could not stop the grinding jealousy the very thought of Myfanwy woke in her breast.

Elspeth took a turn about the courtyard. In the summer it would be warm here, she thought, sheltered from much of the wind and heady with the scents of lilac and roses. But today it was colder than she had realised, despite the pale sun breaking through the clouds. She shivered, deciding to go back inside the house.

At the foot of the stairs leading back to her own apartments, Elspeth hesitated and then turned aside. Alvar had taken her over most of the house himself, showing her the grand chambers used for entertaining company, seldom used since his father's time, and the smaller rooms kept for private use. The manor house was an odd mixture of old and new, one wing of it having been almost entirely rebuilt after a fire some years previously. The old wings had many twists and turns, with steep, winding stone steps leading to the upper chambers, much like Murran Castle; but the new rooms had been built for comfort in the modern fashion, with panelled walls in place of rough-hewn stone and marbled floors.

One wing ran adjacent to the cliff edge, and from those windows you could look out over the sea. But a stout, outer wall separated the house from the sheer face of the cliffs, except in the case of the sea tower which seemed to stand almost alone on a spur of rock projecting out from the rest.

A heavy stone arch curved over the worn steps leading to the tower, and there were signs that the stonework was crumbling. They had passed the outside of the tower one day as they walked in the grounds, and Alvar warned Elspeth against venturing there.

Elspeth gave her word easily, for she saw no reason why she should wish to visit the sea tower. It was obviously in a state of decay, and, besides, there was a rather depressing aura surrounding it. She had felt it as they passed, and she noticed that Alvar felt it too. He had seemed to hurry her on as though he could not bear the sight of the crumbling walls.

Lost in her thoughts, Elspeth turned into a long, dim passage without realising where she was going. It was not until she reached a flight of worn steps, winding upwards into the gloom, that she realised where she was. Somehow she had mistaken the way and taken the passage leading to the sea tower. She stopped, giving a little shiver, and wondering what had made her turn this way. She was about to retrace her steps when she heard a slight noise from the direction of the tower, as though someone was coming down the steps. She frowned, hesitating as the sound grew louder.

Somehow she knew who it would be before Myfanwy came into sight on the curve of the stairway. She halted, obviously surprised to see Elspeth standing there. For a few moments they stared at each other in open hostility, neither of them able to hide their mutual dislike in the shock of the unexpected meeting.

Myfanwy recovered first. 'Is there something I can do for you, my lady?' she asked, her hard, beautiful face twisted with hatred. 'Have you perhaps lost your way?'

Elspeth's eyes darkened with anger, her fierce pride stung by the mocking tone in the other woman's voice. 'What are you doing in the sea tower?' she demanded. 'Do you not know it is forbidden to go there?'

An amused smile hovered about Myfanwy's full, sensual mouth. 'Forbidden to you perhaps—but not to me,' she said. 'I go where I please in Lord Alvar's house. Anywhere . . .'

Elspeth's cheeks burned at the insinuation in Myfanwy's words. Losing her temper, she rushed at her and struck her hard across the face. 'How dare you say such things to me?' she cried furiously. 'You had best keep your place or—or I will have you beaten.'

Myfanwy received the blow without flinching, her smile growing more insolent as she saw Elspeth's fury. She tossed back her flaming red hair, the angry mark blazing on her white skin. 'I think not, my lady,' she said, her voice husky with laughter. 'Not while my lord still needs me. Ask him to punish me and see how he answers you.' Her green eyes glowed with malice in the cat-like face. 'You are but a passing phase, a pretty toy he will tire of soon enough. Then he will come back to me—as he always does.'

Elspeth gave a strangled cry, realising that by losing her temper she had laid herself open to the other woman's jibes. There was no way she could win this argument, for Myfanwy was speaking the truth. Alvar would not send her away, he had made that plain from the start. He refused to tell Elspeth why, and she was afraid to press him too far.

Raising her head proudly, she looked into Myfanwy's face. 'I do not know why Alvar lets you stay here,' she said, forcing herself to speak calmly though she longed to tear out those curious green eyes with her nails. 'But it is not because he desires to lie with you. He will never return to your bed: he has given his word.'

Myfanwy's lips curved into a sneer. 'And you believe him? What a child you are. He has already lain with me since his return.'

Elspeth's face paled. 'You are lying!' she cried, feeling as though a dagger had been plunged into her breast. 'I do not believe you.'

'No?' Myfanwy arched her brow mockingly. 'Would you believe it if I gave you proof?'

'Proof—what proof?' Elspeth dug her nails into the palms of her hands, forcing herself to stay calm. She must not let the other woman see her agony!

Myfanwy's eyes narrowed. 'Tonight, after supper, tell Alvar you are tired and want to retire. Go up to your room and wait until the hour-glass turns for the second time, then come back here and stand at the foot of the stairs. If what you see then does not convince you I speak the truth, you are even more of a fool than I thought you.'

Elspeth stared at her suspiciously. 'You will trick him into coming here with you.'

Myfanwy laughed softly. 'So—you are afraid to learn the truth. You know it already in your heart.'

'You are a liar,' Elspeth whispered through bloodless lips. 'I will come tonight—to prove you lie.'

'And you will not tell him of our meeting?' Myfanwy watched her closely. 'If you do he will suspect a trap and you will never know the truth.'

'I shall not tell him,' Elspeth said quietly, finding it hard not to scream her agony aloud. Her nails had broken through the skin of her palms, but she did not notice the smears of blood on her fingertips as she walked away, leaving Myfanwy staring after her with a mocking smile on her lips.

Elspeth moved through the house like a ghost, seeking the sanctuary of her own apartments. She felt as though she was being torn apart, her body raked with unbearable pain. It couldn't be true. It just couldn't be true! All those nights of unbridled, passionate loving could not mean so little to Alvar that he would leave her arms for Myfanwy. And yet he would not send her away—why?

Mally looked at Elspeth's ashen face, the gown she had been brushing falling to the floor as she rushed to help her mistress who seemed about to collapse.

'What is it, my lady?' she asked, catching Elspeth's hand and chafing it between her own. Then she saw the blood stains. 'You look like death—and you have blood on your hands. What is the matter, my lady?'

Elspeth ignored her anxious questions, twisting her hands away impatiently. She looked at Mally, her eyes dark pools of agony. 'Do you know the sea tower?' she asked, her voice so cold and unlike itself that Mally was shocked into silence.

She nodded. 'I have passed it on my way to the kitchens. They say it is dangerous . . .'

'But some go there, do they not?' Elspeth's eyes blazed suddenly.

Mally seemed uncomfortable. 'I do not know, my lady.'

'Do not lie to me, Mally. I will have the truth from you.'

Mally averted her eyes, gazing down at the floor. 'I have seen . . . Lord Alvar coming from there once,' she said reluctantly.

'And?' Elspeth demanded imperiously, in a manner worthy of the late Earl of Murran himself.

Mally quailed before her wrath. 'Please, my lady, do not make me tell you. I swore I would not . . .' she broke off, giving a little scream as Elspeth slapped her. 'He—he was with her, my lady . . .'

Mally was staring at her with big, hurt eyes, and Elspeth regretted the impulse which had made her strike out, wanting to inflict pain in her own agony. That agony was tearing her apart, making her bleed inside. Her eyes had a queer blind look as she stared unseeingly at Mally.

'Go now,' she whispered, her voice strangely calm and devoid of all emotion. 'I am sorry I hurt you.'

Mally opened her mouth to protest, the shock she had felt on receiving the first blow Elspeth had ever offered melting in a rush of sympathy. She put out her hand to touch her mistress, but at a flash of fire from Elspeth's eyes, she gave a little cry and ran from the room.

Alvar and his men were in good spirits. Having enjoyed a fair day's sport with the young kestrel, they had encountered a wandering minstrel on their return to the manor and carried him back with them to entertain them while they supped. He was a fair youth with a clear, sweet voice and a pretty face.

Listening to his songs of love, Elspeth was reminded of Philip Rathbone. Philip, who was dead because he had dared to stand in Alvar's way. She pushed away her wine goblet, feeling the choicest of wines would be as vinegar in her mouth tonight.

Alvar looked at her, an odd expression in his eyes. 'Are you unwell, Elspeth?' he asked. 'I thought our young friend's songs would please you.'

Elspeth hid her trembling hands beneath the table, determined not to give way to her emotions before the assembled company. Any quarrel she had with Alvar must take place in private, not here in the great hall in full view of his men. She would not shame him though he shamed her with his whore.

'I—I am a little tired, my lord,' she said, avoiding his eyes. 'I pray you—give me leave to retire.'

Alvar furrowed his brow. 'You are not angry because I left you alone today to go hawking, are you? I would have taken you with me, but you were sleeping soundly.'

Elspeth refused to meet his eyes, willing herself to control the surge of anger his words aroused in her. How dare he accuse her when he was betraying her with every breath he drew?

'No, I am not angry because you left me alone. I have

a headache and I would like to rest.'

Alvar stood up. 'If you are really ill I shall come with you. Osric has some knowledge of the physician's art—perhaps he should attend you?'

'No!' Elspeth felt she could bear no more of it. 'Do not fuss so, my lord. It is merely the natural time for a woman—must I say more?'

Alvar seemed relieved. He bent to kiss her hand, his eyes conveying a false message of love and concern. 'Forgive me, I was over anxious and stupid. Go to your bed, then. I will not disturb you.'

'Thank you,' the words almost choked her.

Alone in her chamber, she watched the grains of sand trickling through the hour glass in the flickering candle-light, feeling as though her life's blood was draining with them. At last she stood up and went from the room, carrying the heavy, silver candlestick with her. Guarding its flame with her hand, she walked slowly towards the passage which led to the sea tower, her face as still and cold as death.

When she reached the foot of the winding stairway, Elspeth blew out the candle, standing in the dark. For what seemed an eternity she stood there unmoving, waiting in silence and in dread. Then, when she felt she could bear it no longer, she heard a sound: the sound of voices and footsteps ringing on stone. Faint at first, but becoming louder as they drew nearer.

Now there was a yellow glow as a flickering torch pierced the gloom; and in the sudden light Alvar's face appeared, gleaming palely above his shadowed, black form. He came into view first, bearing the torch, and behind him Myfanwy. She said something, laughing huskily in her throat. He paused on the stair to look back at her, a question in his eyes; and in that moment Myfanwy leant towards him and kissed his lips.

Elspeth gave a cry which was half anger, half despair. Dropping the heavy candlestick with an echoing clang on the stone floor, she turned and fled back the way she had come, scraping her hands on rough walls as she stumbled blindly through the enveloping blackness. Once she thought she heard Alvar call her name, but she did not falter; following her instinct, she blundered on until she reached the main part of the house. Here torches flared in sconces on the walls, lighting the darkness. A servant gaped after her as she rushed past him, disappearing into the upper reaches of the house.

In her bedchamber at last, she leant against the door, pressing it shut with her back, gasping for breath. Mally came in to look at her with wide, frightened eyes, not daring to approach.

'Get out!' Elspeth screamed, half out of her mind in her agony. 'Leave me alone. Leave me alone!'

Mally hovered uncertainly, but as Elspeth's eyes flashed a warning, she gave a smothered sob and ran from the room, too bewildered to know what she ought to do. She had never seen her mistress in such a state, and though she longed to help her, she was frightened to try.

Elspeth hugged her arms about herself, bending over double as the pain ripped through her. She felt as though her body was on fire, pierced by a thousand tiny needles. She wanted to scream and scream, but her lips moved and no sound came. She was dying—dying!

The door to Alvar's room opened and he came in. She stared at him, a red mist of hatred blotting out all reason. 'Go away,' she hissed. 'Go back to your whore!'

Alvar moved nearer, his face a cold, unreadable mask. 'You little fool,' he said. 'Can you not see she planned it all?'

Elspeth's head shot up, her eyes glittering. 'Oh yes, she planned it. I know that well enough—but you need not have gone to her. Nor is it the first time; Mally has seen you with her. Do you deny you have been there with her before this night?'

Alvar shook his head wearily. 'I cannot deny it since you know it to be true—but it is not what you think,

Elspeth, believe me. You promised to trust me, yet you spied on me—you lied to me, letting me think you were sick.'

'I am sick—sick to my stomach with your lies and your cheating,' Elspeth cried, her voice like the rasp of a whip. 'I promised to trust you until you gave me cause to do otherwise . . .'

'Elspeth, listen to me.' Alvar came towards her, but she whirled away, eyes blazing.

'Do not touch me—not ever again.'

Alvar halted, looking at her uncertainly. 'What do you mean? You are my wife . . .'

'And your property,' Elspeth said bitterly, tasting the gall in her throat. 'I know well that you do not let go once you own—but if you touch me again I shall kill myself. I would rather die than share you with her.'

'Elspeth . . .' Alvar's eyes were filled with horror, a look of such agony on his face that her heart stopped for a second. 'Elspeth, you cannot mean it. Please do not say it . . .'

Elspeth looked into his eyes and he saw the coldness in her. 'Touch me and see, my lord. I cannot prevent you from forcing me to submit—but it will be for the last time. Your kisses would make me vomit, just the sight of you makes my stomach churn. The very thought of lying with you makes me feel unclean . . .'

'Enough!' A shuttered look had come over Alvar's face, blocking out all trace of emotion. 'You have made your feelings very clear. Do not distress yourself, I shall not bother you again. Goodnight, madam, forgive me for having intruded upon you.'

Elspeth stared at him in dismay, feeling a terrible agony of loss. She wanted to call him back at once, but her pride would not let her. She watched in silence as he turned and walked from the room. Then she sank to her knees, burying her head in her hands as she wept.

CHAPTER TWELVE

ELSPETH shivered, pulling her velvet mantle closer around her thickening body. She had been for some time standing, staring out at the sea, watching the grey, foaming water spend itself against the treacherous rocks below. Of late she had been here again and again in her loneliness, always turning back to retrace her steps before she reached the long passage leading to the sea tower.

It was four months now since Alvar left for Henry's court, bidding her a curt farewell the morning after their quarrel with no mention of when he would return. Having spent a miserable night alone with her tears, Elspeth would have mended the breach between them if he had given her half a chance, but his coldness had sealed her lips, making it impossible for her to speak. In the empty days and nights which followed his departure, Elspeth had time to look deep within her own heart. Gradually the bitterness she had felt in the heat of anger faded to an aching sense of loss. She began to question her own actions—had she been right to condemn him without a hearing? Had he really betrayed her, or had she let herself be duped by the scheming woman who had set out to destroy her from the start?

At first her pride would not let her admit that she might have acted unfairly: it was she who had been wronged! Alvar should have sent his former mistress away at once. If he loved Elspeth he would not expect her to live under the same roof as that woman! Why should he let her stay—unless it was because he wanted to lie with her?

And yet he had asked her to trust him; he had begged her not to hate him. 'Do not hate me—or you cast me back into Hell,' he had said, and she remembered the pain in his eyes. Was he in Hell even now?

Sometimes Elspeth felt that she was trapped in her own private hell. The bad dreams had come back since he no longer slept at her side. Often she would wake screaming his name, but he was not there to comfort her.

As the days and nights passed into weeks and then months, Elspeth felt the pain of her husband's loss increasingly. Now she began to bitterly regret the terrible things she had said to him on the night she drove him from her room. She had been wild with rage and agony, hardly knowing what she said, regretting the cruel words almost as soon as they were uttered. Now she remembered their passionate love-making, Alvar's tenderness, and the laughter. Sleepless nights followed hard on lonely days in relentless succession, until, at last, she was forced to admit that her life was a barren waste without him. And in that moment she knew that she was ready to go to him on his terms. She had no pride left.

Alvar was the father of the child quickening in her womb. He was her love, her heart, her reason for being. Without him she was an empty shell.

Since Alvar's departure, Myfanwy had never bothered to come near Elspeth. Perhaps she was satisfied now that she had achieved her purpose. She seemed to lead her own life, independent of the household, keeping herself aloof and secret. The other servants respected her but held their distance, obeying her orders in sullen silence. That her rival was not liked by the rest of the household became quickly apparent to Elspeth; for they needed no urging to transfer their allegiance to Alvar's wife. Perhaps they sensed, as servants will, that Myfanwy had caused trouble between their lord and his wife; and they silently ranged themselves behind Elspeth, speaking in low whispers of the change in the beautiful young woman who had captured their sympathy.

Now Elspeth decided that she must seek Myfanwy out. She had to know the truth of what had happened that night. The agony of uncertainty was slowly killing her, draining her of the will to live. Of what use would it be to ask his forgiveness and offer her love if he did not want either one?

Her feet dragged unwillingly as she walked the length of the cold, dark passage leading to the sea tower. At the foot of the winding stairs she paused, hesitating even now. Would Myfanwy tell her the truth? Could Elspeth bear it if she taunted her with Alvar's faithlessness again? And yet she had to ask!

She walked slowly up the stairs, her heart thumping so madly that she felt sick and faint. The stone steps stretched upwards in a sharp spiral, curling towards the crenellated battlements Elspeth had seen from the windows of the new wing. From these it must be possible to see far out to sea, for the spur jutted out right over the rocks and the wild water below.

Suddenly, at a turn in the stairs, she saw a solid oak door set into a recess. She stared at it in surprise. It was quite small: Alvar would have to stoop to enter. She thought it seemed a strange place for Myfanwy to choose as her love-nest, more like a prison than a bedchamber.

Elspeth hovered uncertainly outside the door—should she knock or march straight in and demand the truth? Her hand moved towards it, then she saw that there was no latch, merely a large, iron lock. She took a deep breath and reached out to knock, then she let her hand fall to her side. She was wasting her time: Myfanwy would never admit that Alvar had not lain with her. It was foolish even to ask, it would only invite her scorn. She should not have come.

About to turn away, Elspeth heard a slight noise from behind the door. She jerked back quickly, wanting to escape before Myfanwy discovered her there. Then she heard another sound, a sound which made the hairs on the back of her neck prickle. She shivered, wondering if it was the wind or her imagination. Surely Myfanwy had not made that cry! It was the tortured cry of a wounded animal. As she hesitated, shivering, a despairing scream rent the silence. Suddenly, Elspeth was seized by an unreasoning fear of whatever had made that horrible noise. Pressing her hand against her mouth to prevent herself crying out, she turned and fled back the way she had come, not stopping until she reached her own apartments.

Mally came rushing at her, startled by the stricken look on Elspeth's face. 'Whatever is it, my lady?' she asked, helping her to sit down. 'You are shaking all over.'

'I—I am well enough now,' Elspeth said, half ashamed of her foolish panic. 'It was nothing but folly. I went to the sea tower. I wanted to speak with Myfanwy and . . .'

'And you heard the raven she keeps there screaming, I suppose.' Mally grinned, shaking her head in mock reproof. 'Oh, my lady, why did you go there? Giving yourself such a fright—and all for nothing!'

Elspeth stared at her, disbelief in her eyes. 'A raven—you say it was a raven I heard? It could not have been. It was terrible—unearthly! You just cannot imagine it.'

Mally laughed. 'So I have heard tell. They say it sounds like a demon from Hell—but it is only her pet raven, my lady. I have seen her taking it food, and she told me herself what it was for.'

Elspeth gave her a wan smile. 'Yes, I suppose it could have been a bird screeching. That tower is so—so chilling somehow. I must have let my imagination run away with me.'

'It is your delicate condition,' Mally said primly, pursing her lips in disapproval. 'You should not wander about alone the way you do. It isn't good for you to spend all your time moping. Why do you not write to your sister and beg her to visit you? It is but a day's good journey . . .'

Elspeth shook her head. 'No, I cannot. Sir Harold is still confined to his bed. I could not ask her to leave him while he is ill. Perhaps later—when he is recovered . . .'

Mally suddenly clapped her hand to her mouth. 'Oh, my lady, forgive me!' she cried in dismay. 'There is a letter come for you this hour from Lord Alvar and I forgot—seeing you in such a state . . .'

Elspeth started, her heart pulsing rapidly. 'A letter—from my lord? Where is it? Give it to me at once!'

'I have not got it, my lady. The messenger vows he will only give it into your hands. He was ready to search the house for you, but I bade him wait in the great chamber . . .'

'Then find him and bring him to me immediately. Go on! What are you waiting for?' Elspeth jumped to her feet impatiently. 'Must I go myself?'

'Bide you here, my lady, and rest. I will bring him to you myself—though he's a strange, nasty creature . . .'

'Mally!'

'Yes, my lady. I go. I go . . .'

Mally hurried from the room, while Elspeth began to pace about the floor in a fever of impatience. A letter from Alvar! He had written to her at last . . . She stopped her pacing in surprise as Mally returned with Alvar's messenger in tow.

'Quinn!' she exclaimed in astonishment as she saw his ugly little face grinning at her. 'Oh, Quinn, I am so happy to see you!'

The dwarf gave a cackle of delighted laughter. 'Have I suddenly become tall and handsome, lady? Or could it be that I have something you covet?'

Elspeth flushed. 'Is—is my lord well?' she asked, her voice dropping to a whisper.

Quinn tipped his head to one side, his eyes glittering with sly humour. 'I have known him in better temper—but his tongue is as sharp as ever and he still has all his limbs. When he bade me bring this letter to you he was preparing for the battle against the Yorkist rebels . . .'

'The Yorkist rebels?' Elspeth's face drained of colour. 'I have heard nothing of this—the last I heard was that His Majesty had quelled the rumours about the young Earl of Warwick by taking him from the Tower and showing him to the people.'

Quinn gave a harsh laugh. 'Then you know nothing, lady. The pretender, Lambert Simnel, has been crowned King of England in that heathen land of the Irish; and the Lady Margaret of Burgundy has sent Lord Lincoln with a large force to aid the rebels in their attempt to dislodge Henry Tudor from the throne.'

Elspeth drew a deep breath, a spasm of fear turning her legs to water. 'And—Alvar will fight at Henry's side.' She closed her eyes as the tears threatened. Alvar was going to war—and they had parted in bitterness! If he should die he would never know how much she loved him. How much she regretted their quarrel. She held out her hand to Quinn. 'Give me his letter, I pray you—then leave me, both of you. I will speak with you again later, Quinn. Mally, I will send for you in a little while.'

'Yes, my lady.'

'I will carry an answer should you wish it, lady,' Quinn said, his eyes bright with an unspoken question.

Elspeth nodded, hardly able to contain her fever of impatience. 'Perhaps. Leave me now, I beg you.'

Quinn bowed and followed Mally from the room, closing the door behind them.

Elspeth sat down, turning the precious parchment in her hands and staring at the bold seal. Her fingers shaking, she broke it open, spreading out the folds. Alvar had written in a clear, firm hand, beginning simply:

'Madam, I feel it my duty to write this letter to you since I go to meet the rebels tomorrow, and only God knows if we shall ever see each other again in this life. Quinn, who has been a friend to us both in the past, will have brought this to you. It needs no answer, but for your comfort I would have you keep him with you until I return. You may trust him with your life. I tell you this, though you may not choose to believe it since he comes from me, and I know you have learned to hate me.

'But I shall not reproach you for your lack of trust—for I deserved no more than I received at your hands. I have most grievously wronged you, madam, though not in the manner you accused me of. As God is my witness, I did not betray our love, if love it was. When you know all the truth you may believe it was the Devil's work, and who shall say you are wrong? But I will not trouble you with it now, for if I go to my grave I shall carry the secret with me. If that should happen, put yourself in Quinn's hands. He will know what must be done.

'I pray God—or the Devil—may grant me life for long enough to make reparation for the wrong I have done you. I shall not ask forgiveness. It would be useless. Alvar.'

Elspeth stared at the words Alvar had penned, tears blurring them into a senseless mass. He had written so coldly, with no hint of the reconciliation she had hoped for. He wrote of dying as though his death was of no importance—almost as though he would welcome it.

He spoke of reparation for the wrong he had done her—what wrong? What did he mean? It was her own, wicked jealousy which had driven them apart! He had asked for her trust and she had behaved like a foolish, peevish child, allowing Myfanwy to blind her with malicious lies. Alvar had not lain with her: he had kept his word. There was some other reason for his visit to the sea tower—some trickery of Myfanwy's no doubt.

What was this great wrong he must make reparation for? she wondered, brushing away her tears. Surely nothing could be so terrible that it could come between them? Nothing would ever part them again, she vowed, nothing but death! Suddenly she was overcome with a desperate longing to see him again, to hold him in her arms and beg for his forgiveness.

Elspeth pressed her lips to his signature, tears trickling down her cheeks. 'Forgive me, my love,' she sobbed. 'Oh, forgive me, Alvar.'

She slipped to her knees, clasping her hands in fervent prayer. 'Bring him back to me,' she begged. 'Oh, God, do not punish me further for my sins. Take pity and bring him back to me. I beseech you . . .'

Her prayers were answered: Alvar had come home. But as Elspeth looked at his grey face she felt a cold dread clutch her heart. He was close to death, his eyes closed, a deep wound in his side still bleeding intermittently. Was this her punishment? Had he been restored to her only to die before her anguished eyes?

She turned her tear-blinded eyes towards the men who had carried him home. 'Take him to his chamber,' she said. 'I shall nurse him myself.'

One of the soldiers stared at her strangely, a half protest on his lips; but Elspeth had eyes only for her lord and she did not notice. It was not until the men had laid Alvar on the bed and departed that she saw one of them had lingered after his companions.

'Yes—was there something?' she asked, wishing him gone so that she could be alone with her love.

'Do you know me, my lady?'

Something in his voice made her look at him more closely, and she saw that it was the man, Firkin, who had once served her so faithfully. 'Firkin? Forgive me—I did not notice you. How may I serve you?'

Firkin studied her face intently. 'You once said you would tell me when it was time—is it time, my lady? I cannot let you do it! I know you have cause enough to hate him—but he does not deserve so cruel an end . . .'

Elspeth stared at him, her eyes widening with horror. 'Do you believe I mean him harm? Do you think I would hasten his death?'

A hot colour swept up the soldier's neck, staining his cheeks. 'I thought you hated him—I thought 'twas why you sent him away from you, using your beauty to torment his soul—but 'tis not so, I can see that now. Forgive me, my lady, I misjudged you. I have come to respect Lord Alvar—and, yes, I will say it, to love him as all his men do. He is a brave man. He has the strength of ten men in battle, and yet he can be merciful—even gentle . . .' His skin was now a dark red and he could not finish.

Elspeth nodded, smiling. 'I see that he has won your heart, sir. Should I blame you for seeking to protect the man I love? Pray for him, Firkin—and for me.'

The soldier inclined his head slightly. 'I will,' he said; but Elspeth hardly heard him.

'Hot water, Mally,' she said, as her maid hovered by the bedside. 'We need water, salves and fresh linen. His wound is weeping again.'

'It needs to be cauterised,' Mally replied, her face grim. 'It is the only way to stop the bleeding.'

Elspeth stared at her, whitefaced. 'Then it must be done . . .'

'I will do it, my lady,' Firkin spoke from behind her. 'I have seen it done many times. You, girl, make the fire ready while I remove his clothes. You had best summon help—he may come to himself when the iron touches him.'

Mally nodded, hurrying away to do his bidding. Elspeth could only hover at the bedside, helping when she could as Firkin stripped the blood-soaked tunic from Alvar piece by piece. She smothered a gasp as she saw the deep gash in his side, the flesh purplish-black and crusted at the edges with dried blood.

Firkin's face was stern as he heard the smothered gasp, hiding the emotion he felt inside. 'It is a serious wound, my lady, but he is a strong man. Do not despair—if we can stop the bleeding he has a fair chance of recovery.'

Elspeth nodded, not trusting herself to reply. She wrung out a cloth in cold water, sponging away the fresh blood oozing from the wound. She prayed to God he was right—but Alvar had lost so much blood! She took a grip on her emotions as Mally returned with two of Alvar's men.

Firkin looked at her sharply. 'Perhaps you should leave us, my lady—this will not be pleasant.'

Elspeth shook her head, feeling that she could not bear to leave her husband's side even for a while. She raised her eyes to him, pale but determined. 'I will stay with him,' she said.

Firkin shrugged. Realising she would not be swayed, he turned his attention to the business in hand. Having warned the soldiers to hold Alvar steady in case he should rouse and do himself more injury, he took the cauterising iron, the tip of which was smoking hot, from Mally, his face grim.

Alvar had lain unmoving all this time, his eyes firmly closed and only the slight, uneven rhythm of his breathing to show he still lived. But as the iron touched his flesh he suddenly cried out, writhing in a paroxysm of agony; and it took the combined strength of both soldiers to hold him down.

His eyes flew open, staring wildly but without registering what he saw. He was like a wounded beast, conscious only of the unendurable pain as the heat seared his skin.

It was over very quickly; but to Elspeth, watching her husband writhe in mindless agony, it was more terrible than she could ever have imagined.

The ordeal seemed to have exhausted the last of Alvar's strength, for he fell back against the pillows lifelessly. Elspeth gave a little scream and ran to his side, her eyes darting accusingly at Firkin.

'You have killed him!'

'Nay, my lady, he has merely lost his senses for a time. It usually happens that way—be thankful he knows nothing of the pain while he is in this state. It will be worse when he comes to himself.'

'Firkin speaks the truth, my lady,' Mally said. 'See—Lord Alvar still breathes; and the bleeding has stopped.'

Elspeth looked at Alvar and saw the slight movement of his chest. 'Thank God!' she whispered, her hand reaching shakily to touch his sweat-ridden brow. Then she looked at Firkin. 'Forgive me—I did not mean to offend you, sir. You have done me a great service.'

Firkin shook his head. 'It matters not. There is no more you can do, but watch over him and wait . . .'

'And pray,' Elspeth said. 'I can pray for God's mercy.'

Elspeth bent over the bed as Alvar began to thrash feverishly again, sponging his heated brow with a cool cloth. For ten days and nights now he had been in a delirium, tossing wildly from side to side, often starting up as though he would leave his bed. Sometimes he would lie down again at the sound of Elspeth's voice, apparently comforted; but at others it took a man's strength to restrain him.

Two nights ago, Myfanwy had come to the door of his chamber, bearing a pitcher and asking to see Elspeth. At first Mally had tried to send her away, but she burst into the room, staring at Alvar's pain-racked body with wild eyes.

'What do you want?' Elspeth asked, anger rising in her. 'How dare you come here!'

Myfanwy held out the pitcher. 'This will save him . . .' she broke off as she saw the hatred in Elspeth's eyes. 'Oh, I know you hate me—but I do not care what you think of me. Will you let him die when you could save him?'

Elspeth stared at her. 'How do I know it is not poison?'

Myfanwy laughed mockingly. 'If I offered it to you you might have cause to doubt, my lady.' She lifted it to her lips and drank deeply, then held it out to Elspeth once more. 'Please take it—for his sake.'

'Very well.' Elspeth took it reluctantly.

'Make him swallow some of it every four hours,' Myfanwy said, then she was gone.

For a few moments Elspeth had remained staring after her, then she poured some of the mixture into a cup and, calling Mally to help her, she held it to Alvar's lips.

Elspeth had nursed him throughout the ten days herself, leaving him only when Mally forced her to rest. She could not bear to be away from him, sleeping only fitfully in her dread of being roused with news of his death.

Thankfully, his wound had at last begun to show signs of mending, though it would be a long time in healing. But if only the fever would abate, Alvar might recover his strength.

'You must not die,' she whispered fiercely, tears catching in her voice as she bent over him. 'I cannot bear it if you die!'

Suddenly she could bear the pain no longer. If Alvar was going to die she must hold him in her arms just once more. She eased herself carefully on to the bed beside him, laying her face against his bare shoulder, comforted by the warmth of his body. He had ceased his restless tossing for the moment and seemed to be more peaceful at last. Curled at his side, Elspeth relaxed as she had not been able to in her own bed; and then, worn out with watching and anxiety, she slept.

'Elspeth?'

The voice against her ear ruffled the chords of memory like a gentle breeze, bringing her instantly awake. For a moment she stared sleepily at her husband, smiling, forgetful of all that had happened since the last time she wakened at his side; then she suddenly realised that his cool, blue eyes were regarding her lucidly, without a trace of the fever which had possessed him so long.

'The fever has gone,' she said, blushing as she sat up.

'I must have fallen asleep—forgive me. Have you been awake long?'

Alvar made a slight, negative movement, his eyes following her as she left the bed to pour water into a goblet. But as she returned, slipping her hand behind his head to lift him, his hand shot out and gripped her wrist.

'No—not yet,' he muttered in a hoarse whisper. 'I have been ill—what happened?'

'You were wounded. Your men brought you home ten days ago. We had to cauterise the wound to stop the bleeding, but it is mending slowly. You have been in a fever ever since . . .'

'And you—why are you here with me?' Alvar's fingers tightened about her wrist, his eyes boring into her.

'Where else should I be?' Elspeth replied. 'You are my husband; my place is by your side. Come, swallow some water; it will ease your throat.'

Alvar's grip relaxed on her wrist and he swallowed obediently, falling back against the pillows as though the effort had been too much for him.

'I may have been ill but my wits have not deserted me,' he said after a moment, his mouth curving in a sneer. 'Why do you waste your time in caring for a man you hate? Why did you not let me die, Elspeth?'

Elspeth put down the goblet, her hands trembling. 'I do not hate you, my lord.'

'No?' He gave a derisive laugh. 'Then you are a fool, madam—or does it please you to see me lying here, helpless?'

Elspeth's face was very pale. 'I cannot blame you for your bitterness, my lord. I behaved like a stupid, wilful child. I was jealous when I had no need to be. I can only beg you humbly to forgive me.'

Alvar's mouth curved in a wry smile. 'Me—forgive you?' he asked. 'What new game is this, Elspeth? Would you have me come crawling to your feet to beg for your favours so that you can cast me back into Hell when it pleases you? Is that why you kept me alive—so that you can savour the sweetness of your revenge?'

Elspeth flinched at the bitterness in his voice. 'You wrong me, my lord. Do not punish me further for my foolishness, I beg you. I have suffered enough these past months since you left. As God is my witness, I want only to be your wife, to return to the happiness we once knew—if you will have me.'

'Happiness? I have no right to happiness.' Alvar moved his hand wearily. 'Even if you meant it—it is too late. Too late. I should never have brought you here. Go! Leave this very day, Elspeth. Leave me while I am too weak to stop you. Go before I change my mind—before I drag you down into Hell with me.'

Elspeth moved closer to the bed. Lifting his hand, she placed it on her swollen belly. 'Have you no eyes, my lord? Would you send me away when your child grows in my womb? If I have killed your love—then let me stay for my child's sake.'

'My child?' Alvar's eyes suddenly blazed with new life. 'My child, Elspeth? You would not lie to me?'

'Look at me, my lord. Touch me. Can you not see that I am telling the truth?'

Alvar's eyes travelled over her, a look of wonder passing across his face. 'It is true,' he whispered, speaking more to himself than Elspeth. 'Then you cannot go—you are bound to me for good or ill . . .'

Elspeth sat down beside him. Taking his hand in hers, she laid it against her cheek. 'I love you,' she said. 'Do not speak of sending me away, I beg you.'

'Love, hate—where is the dividing line, Elspeth? How strong is your love, I wonder. You sent me away from you for an imagined wrong—yet I have done you a much greater wrong than you know.'

'I was a foolish child—but I have learned to be a woman. I know now that my life is nothing without you. Speak no more of reparation, I want only your love.'

'That has been yours since we first met, Elspeth.' Alvar sighed wearily. 'I asked you to trust, and yet I would not trust you. There is so much I should have told you long ago—but I am tired and the tale is bitter. You shall decide if your love will hold once you hear it—but it will keep for another day . . .' His eyelids flickered and closed.

Elspeth bent over him, brushing her lips over his lightly. 'Rest now, my dearest lord,' she said.

CHAPTER THIRTEEN

ELSPETH sighed and laid aside her stitchery, feeling unable to settle to her work. She stood up, easing herself. Her back was aching and she could feel the child stirring in her womb. Yet neither of these things was at the root of her uneasiness. Today Alvar had gone riding with his men for the first time since he recovered from his injury; and though Elspeth knew his wound was almost completely healed, she could not help being anxious. In vain she had pleaded with him to wait a few more days. He was restless, moody and bored with long weeks of enforced idleness. Not all her pleas could hold him back.

'I need the exercise,' he said, scowling at her. 'Hush your scolding, Elspeth, lest I beat you for being a nagging wife.'

She had just smiled and shaken her head, knowing he was merely mocking her; for nothing could have exceeded his care for her since his own recovery. Within a few days of the fever subsiding he was his own master once more, refusing to keep to his bed but insisting that she stayed in hers until well into the mornings.

'Anyone would think I had been ill!' Elspeth complained peevishly; but it was useless to argue with him and their relationship was too fragile for her to press him too far. So she did as he bid her; and she let him go with his men, though she would be in agony until he returned safely.

At least there was no pressing need for him to return to court, she thought thankfully. The rebels had been defeated; and once again Henry Tudor had shown his keen wit. Instead of putting the boy, Lambert Simnel, to death, he had set him to work in the kitchens of the palace, thereby turning a serious threat into a farce.

It was no use! She could not remain shut up in her rooms while Alvar was gone. The minutes dragged by with leaden feet, each one seeming like an hour. She would go down and walk in the courtyard. She must do something!

Outside in the sunshine, Elspeth breathed deeply, feeling more relaxed. She smiled as the child kicked in her womb. 'Not long now, my love,' she whispered. She was carrying the babe well and her time was creeping nearer. In a few weeks she would give Alvar his son. Perhaps then he would shed the restless mood which possessed him.

Elspeth frowned suddenly. He had never spoken again of her leaving, nor had he attempted to tell her of the wrong he had done her; but somehow she knew it was this which brought on his black moods, and sometimes she thought he was afraid to break his silence. But what was it he feared . . . ?

'My lady—I would speak with you.'

The sound of Myfanwy's voice startled Elspeth. She jumped, spinning round to face the other woman. 'I did not hear you—what do you want?' Elspeth could not hide her hostility, even though she believed that the mixture Myfanwy had given her had helped to ease Alvar's fever.

Myfanwy lowered her eyes, her attitude one of humble respect. 'Forgive me, my lady,' she said. 'I know you hate me, and I cannot blame you. I have deserved your hatred—but I loved Alvar. In my jealousy I tried to destroy you. I was spiteful and cruel. I am sorry I caused you pain.'

'It is no matter. Alvar has come back to me. I carry his child. You are nothing to me now,' Elspeth's voice was harsh, her face hard and unforgiving. 'Do not ask me to forgive you. I shall never forget what you are—nor what you tried to do.'

For a moment there was a gleam of anger in Myfanwy's eyes, but she veiled them quickly with her long lashes, maintaining her air of meekness. 'So be it, my lady. After this day I shall trouble you no more. I am going away—but before I leave, there is something I must tell you . . .'

'Leave?' Elspeth stared at her. 'Are you going from here?'

'Yes. I—I feel my presence here is a burden to you.' Myfanwy's voice was suddenly eager. 'Believe me, my lady, I am truly sorry for all the pain I have caused you. I want—nay, I must make amends. My conscience will not let me go without doing all I can to help you. You are in great danger: there is one who desires your death . . .' She looked over her shoulder fearfully. 'We cannot talk here. You must come with me.'

Elspeth held back suspiciously. 'Come where? Why should I trust you?'

Myfanwy wrung her hands, her eyes rolling wildly. 'How can I make you believe me? For your own sake—for the sake of the child you carry—you must learn Alvar's secret! You must listen—before it is too late!'

Elspeth's heart lurched, beginning to thump madly in her breast. 'Alvar's secret—what do you mean?'

Myfanwy's eyes darted furtively to the windows of the house, as if she was afraid of being seen. 'I dare not tell you here,' she said. 'He would kill me if he knew. I am jealous and spiteful, I admit it—but I am not a wicked woman. I do not want your death on my soul. I beg you to come with me, there is something you must know!'

Elspeth could see that Myfanwy's fear was real, not feigned. She allowed herself to be hurried into the house, still not trusting the other woman but drawn on against her will. She knew without being told that they were going to the sea tower. Somehow, she realised, she had always known that there was some secret locked away in that grim place. She had known but she had blocked it from her mind, afraid of what she might learn if she pressed too far.

At the foot of the worn, stone steps she halted, half-minded to go back even now; but Myfanwy caught her arm, forcing her on. Elspeth was surprised at the other woman's strength. She would have found it difficult to break away from her determined grip in the confined space of the twisting stairway. But as Myfanwy pushed a key in the iron lock, she suddenly pulled back in alarm.

'No, I do not want to go in. I do not want to know . . .'

'Afraid, my lady?' Myfanwy's voice was like the serpent's hiss as she thrust Elspeth through the narrow entrance.

Elspeth stumbled, falling forward down a step and clutching at the stone wall to steady herself. She turned just in time to see the door closing, flinging herself at it in a desperate attempt to hold it back, but she was too late.

'What do you think you are doing? Let me out. Let me out at once!'

From behind the door Myfanwy's laughter echoed mockingly. 'Too late, sweet lady. You are doomed—you and your brat. You thought to take Alvar from me. You persuaded him to banish me—but before I go I shall see you dead.'

'I do not know what you are talking about. I have not asked Alvar to send you away,' Elspeth cried. 'Let me out now and I will not tell him of this trick—they are bound to find me in the end.'

'Oh yes, I shall tell Alvar where you are myself when he returns. I want to see his face—but by then it will be too late.' Myfanwy laughed again chillingly. 'Look behind you, lady. The beast sleeps, but soon it will wake—and then you die . . .'

'Stop trying to frighten me with your tales,' Elspeth shouted, beating her fists against the door. 'I have heard of the pet you keep here. Let me out and stop trying to scare me. Put an end to this nonsense!'

'Nonsense is it?' Myfanwy laughed again. 'You will see soon enough, my lady. Goodbye—think of me when you are longing for death. I am going now.'

Elspeth threw herself at the door, banging on it desperately as she heard the sound of Myfanwy's footsteps retreating. She was going away! 'Come back. Come back this instant!' She gave a choking sob. 'Myfanwy, please stop trying to frighten me. You have had your fun—now let me out. Please, let me out!'

There was no answer. Myfanwy had gone, leaving her in this horrible little room. Elspeth was becoming aware of the stench: it was like rotting vegetables, a sour acrid smell that made her feel sick. It was dark in here too, much darker than on the stairway. There was no window in the room, she realised as her eyes became adjusted to the gloom; what light and air there was came from a grille somewhere above.

She stood with her back pressed against the door, her nerves tingling as she became aware of the heavy air of oppression hanging over the cell-like room. The feeling of menace mounted in her strongly, making her heart thump and her mouth run dry with fear. Then she stiffened as she heard a slight rustling sound from somewhere in the shadows at the far side of the room. A grey, formless shape caught her eyes. It was humped on the floor like a pile of old sacking left to rot. Then, as Elspeth stared disbelievingly, it moved. It seemed to swell and grow larger, rising into the air until it stood upright.

Elspeth swallowed hard, a nameless fear turning her limbs to water as she stared at the thing, echoes of the nightmares which had haunted her for months rearing frighteningly to life. It swayed unsteadily for a few moments, then shuffled forward slowly. It was coming towards her. Her skin prickled with horror as it approached. It moved so slowly, yet it came ever closer. Now she realised that the foul stench in the room emanated from the thing. It was just a grey mass, like rotting rags. Then it raised its head and looked at her, and Elspeth saw the pitiful creature before her had once been a woman.

Elspeth gasped, feeling a thrill of horror run through her. 'Who—who are you?' she whispered through dry lips. 'Why are you here?'

The woman gazed at her from soulless eyes in which there was no flicker of recognition nor understanding. The eyes were as vacant as the grey face. Filthy grey hair matted about the head, falling spikily on to the rags which hung on the emaciated body. The creature moved and breathed, but otherwise it was dead, rotting with disease like a walking corpse.

Elspeth stared at the creature, pity stirring in her heart despite the horror clawing at her belly. While she shrank from contact with the foul thing it had become, she was shocked to the core by the plight of the wretched woman. She crossed herself quickly, her lips moving in silent prayer.

'Oh, my God,' she whispered sickly, her face ashen. 'What can have brought any woman to this?'

A change had come over the creature; from being vacant, the eyes seemed to glitter strangely. Elspeth watched in revulsion as the wretched woman began to mutter and slobber excitedly. She lurched unsteadily towards Elspeth, her hands clutching at Elspeth's gown. Elspeth recoiled, her pity rapidly dissolving into fear as the woman fumbled at her belly, stroking the swollen mound beneath the gown.

Elspeth stood absolutely still, fighting the waves of nausea washing over her as the creature prodded and pawed. The stench of the diseased woman's body rose in her nostrils, making her retch. She dug her nails deep into the palms of her hands, willing herself not to make any sudden movements, praying that Alvar would come. At the moment the creature seemed harmless, even affectionate; but Myfanwy had not been lying. She had brought Elspeth here to die. Remembering the screams she had heard coming from this room, Elspeth knew the creature's mood could change at any time.

Suddenly her straining ears caught the sound of running feet. Someone was coming! Thank God. Thank God! Steadily, smiling reassuringly, she edged away from the door so that its inward thrust should not send her sprawling. The creature was growing more excited, saliva dribbling down its chin as it muttered and pawed at Elspeth's belly.

Then the door was flung open and Quinn came hurtling into the room. 'Get out, my lady!' he shrieked. 'Thank heaven I am in time!'

Elspeth tried to obey, but the creature clutched a handful of her gown, pulling at it savagely. Its playful mood had evaporated at the sight of the dwarf. All at once the creature screamed and dived at Quinn. A knife flashed silver in the gloom, burying itself deep in Quinn's breast. Elspeth found herself free, but still she could not move. She stared in horrified fascination at the startled look on Quinn's face and the blood oozing from the slash in his doublet.

Then the creature turned to look at her, eyes glittering insanely, horrible, bestial grunts issuing from its lips. Elspeth gave a shriek of terror, fleeing towards the door. As she emerged from the gloomy cell, she heard shouts and voices raised in anger. She began to run down the steps, conscious that the creature was following her. As she turned the bend in the stairway, she tripped and catapulted into Alvar's arms.

'Quinn is dead,' she gasped out, shuddering uncontrollably. 'That—that creature killed him.'

Alvar did not answer. For a moment he held her close to him, then he thrust her roughly behind him. Elspeth looked back and saw the creature poised above them on the stairs.

'Go back to your room, Megan,' Alvar said, his voice softly purring as he watched the ragged creature on the stairway. 'Go back and Myfanwy will come to you. No one means you any harm, but you must go back for your own sake.'

Alvar's soft voice seemed to have an almost hypnotic effect on the woman. She whimpered, backing away slowly, never turning her eyes from Alvar.

He moved forward cautiously, keeping up the soft, reassuring litany; persuading, soothing, forcing her back by the sheer strength of his will. Then Myfanwy pushed past Elspeth, her face working with hatred.

'Kill him, Megan!' she screamed. 'Kill! Kill! Kill! He will lock you in that room again. Kill him now!'

The spell was broken. The woman's eyes rolled wildly and she gave a despairing scream; but instead of attacking Alvar, she turned and fled up the stone steps, past the gloomy cell-like room, on up towards the battlements.

'No! No, Megan, no!' Myfanwy screamed, rushing past Alvar before he could guess what she meant to do.

'Come back, Myfanwy, she is dangerous,' Alvar cried, following at a run.

Elspeth climbed the steps more slowly, drawn after them against her will. Outlined against the darkening sky, she saw Myfanwy locked in a desperate struggle with the wretched woman. Then, almost as Alvar reached them, they fell over the edge of the low, protecting wall; their bodies entwined together as they crashed on to the rocks below.

Elspeth reached her husband's side, the sickness rising in her as she saw the red, swirling foam licking about the rocks; watching in numb horror as the water tossed the limp forms high into the air before dragging them under.

'Come away, Elspeth,' Alvar said, forcing her back from the edge. 'Come away—it is over at last.'

Elspeth leant her head against his shoulder, shuddering. She looked up at her husband. 'That poor, mad creature—who was she?'

Alvar held her tighter. 'She was Myfanwy's sister, and . . .'

'And?' Elspeth asked, knowing the answer already.

'And my wife.' Alvar's face was full of pain. 'Do not hate me, Elspeth—listen to my story and do not judge me too harshly.'

'I could never hate you, my dear love,' Elspeth replied. 'I know that whatever you have to tell me will not change my heart. You are not to blame for this, I know it as surely as I know that God has been merciful this day.'

'Thank you.' Alvar smiled sadly, his eyes tender as they rested on her face. 'Come, my beloved, the wind is cold. Let us go below: I will explain as we walk.'

Elspeth nodded, leaning on his arm as he drew her towards the stairway. As they neared the tower room in which Alvar's mad wife had been shut away for so long, a figure emerged and Elspeth saw it was her husband's steward. He looked at Alvar questioningly and Alvar nodded.

'It is over, Osric.'

The steward crossed himself. 'She is at peace, my lord, do not blame yourself. No man could have tried harder to help the poor lady.' He looked at Elspeth oddly. 'Does—does Lady Alvar know?'

'She knows. You must make arrangements for Quinn's body to be carried to his room . . .'

'No need, my lord.' Quinn's voice sounded less than its usual cheery self as he came out of the cell, clutching a cloth to his padded doublet to staunch the wound. 'It takes more than a scratch to kill poor Quinn!'

'Quinn! Oh, Quinn, you are alive!' Elspeth's cry of delight brought a grin to the dwarf's face.

'Take care, lady, else my Lord Alvar will finish what the madwoman began!'

'Aye, that I will.' Alvar agreed, laughing. 'Be off with you, rogue, I shall not waste my sympathy on such a fraud! See the rascal to his bed, Osric—and make sure he stays there.'

Elspeth smiled, leaning into the crook of Alvar's arm as they passed on by. She could still hear Quinn refusing to be helped as they traversed the passage leading back to the main wing of the house.

Alone at last, Alvar halted, gazing down into Elspeth's face. 'If anything had happened to you tonight, I should have wanted to die. It was my fault—I ought to have told you about Myfanwy and Megan long ago. But I was afraid you would leave me if you knew the truth.'

Elspeth shook her head. 'Perhaps I would have at the start—but after you made me your own, I could never have left you in this life. I knew that when we quarrelled—without you I am nothing.' She looked up into his eyes earnestly. 'Will you not tell me the whole now—so that the past can finally be laid to rest?'

'Yes, you must know it all.' Alvar's eyes were dark with remembered pain. 'You know part of it already, for I told you the truth—Megan was my betrothed.'

'I thought it must be so.'

'She was always a gentle, timid girl. Our fathers arranged the marriage when we were both in the cradle—but when the time came, I found it easy to love her. Not as I love you—but enough for contentment's sake . . .'

Elspeth nodded, smiling. 'Do not be anxious, my lord, I am no longer a foolish child. Please tell me everything.'

Alvar touched her cheek. 'Never leave me, Elspeth. Never doubt that I need you.'

Elspeth caught his hand and kissed it. 'As I need you, my lord.'

Alvar nodded, a tiny pulse beating in his throat. 'Her father brought her here for our betrothal: we were to have been married a few weeks later. We were all so happy together—Megan, her father and Myfanwy—and I. Then I was called away urgently to a neighbour's estate. I begged Megan's father to make free of my home while I was gone . . .' Alvar's voice trailed away as though he found it too painful to go on.

'Yes, tell me, my dearest lord—for then it will be truly over,' Elspeth whispered.

'While I was gone, Megan and her father went hawking in the woods: Myfanwy remained in the house because she felt unwell. She told me what had happened when I returned . . .' He took a deep breath. 'One of the grooms had been left for dead, but he managed to crawl to the village and tell his story. Megan's father had been brutally slain with all his servants—and Megan was carried off screaming by Baron Cassell. What Myfanwy did not know was that the Baron had been my father's enemy for many years.'

'Your father was dead—so he took his revenge on you.'

'Yes. He carried Megan off to his stronghold and forced a priest to marry them. He was not content with ravishing her—he wanted a complete revenge. He thought marriage would stop me taking her back. He . . .' Alvar's voice faltered and then grew harsh. 'He raped her, then subjected her to such bestial vileness that, when I brought her back to Alvar, she was shocked rigid. She could not speak for days, and then she would only speak of it to Myfanwy . . .'

'The poor, poor girl,' Elspeth said, her eyes full of pity. 'It was enough to turn anyone's mind.'

Alvar nodded, tight-lipped. 'That is not all . . .' He curled his hands into hard fists, the knuckles gleaming whitely. 'At first she seemed well enough, just shocked and quieter than before. Myfanwy begged me to give her time to recover and I agreed. I wanted only to help her—to wipe the memory of that terrible night from her mind. Then we discovered she was with child. I summoned a priest and we were married with Myfanwy and Osric to witness the ceremony. No one else knew of it . . .'

Elspeth waited in silence for him to recover himself,

then: 'Still Myfanwy begged me to be patient. I agreed. I did not attempt to touch her—it was a marriage in name only. I waited until after the child was born. I did not care that the boy was his—for he was also hers. I was prepared to accept him as my son. But Megan showed no affection for the babe. She would not even look at him. So we fetched a woman from the village to suckle him and he thrived. Perhaps I should have been warned—but how could I have guessed?'

Alvar paused again, obviously finding it difficult to continue. 'Go on, my lord,' Elspeth urged, knowing that he must not falter now if he was ever to be free of the shadow which had haunted him.

Alvar shuddered at the memory he found so horrible he could hardly bear to put it into words. 'One day I went up to the nursery to look at the child—he was a beautiful child. I saw Megan bending over the cradle and I was happy. I believed she had at last accepted him, and I felt that she might now come to terms with what had happened to her—but when I looked into the cot I saw . . . blood.' Alvar's face was grim. 'She had killed her own child.'

'Oh . . .' Elspeth blanched with shock. Never had she expected anything quite as terrible as this! But Alvar was talking again, the words pouring out of him now as if a dam had been released:

'She was laughing. She screamed that she was glad the brat was dead. It was obvious she was insane. At first we kept her locked in her chambers. Sometimes she was docile, sometimes she ripped her clothes and attacked anyone who ventured near her. Myfanwy was the only one who could calm her. At last even she had to give Megan mixtures made of poppy seeds to quieten her. She began to foul her rooms and tear at her skin with her nails—then she started a fire. I carried her out and everyone thought she was dead. I let them believe it and I carried her to the tower in secret, telling only Myfanwy and Osric. I knew the servants said she had the evil eye, and I was afraid one of them would try to kill her when I was away . . .'

'My poor love,' Elspeth said, catching his hand. 'It is over now—she is at peace.'

Alvar nodded grimly. 'Thank God. Sometimes I considered finishing it—one thrust of my sword and it would have all been over. I could not do it, Elspeth. I could not forget what she had once been. I continued to hope that she might recover—and Myfanwy begged me to stay my hand. That was when we became lovers. She offered herself to me and I needed . . . something. At last I could stand the strain no longer and I left Alvar. I went to France and there I met Henry Tudor. I came back to Alvar just before I travelled to Murran Castle for your sister's wedding. Megan was so much worse by that time that I thought she would not live long. When I asked your father for your hand in marriage I expected to be free to wed you in a year. It was only Myfanwy's determination which kept her sister alive—for the doctors we brought to her at the start could do nothing to help her.'

Elspeth looked at him sadly. 'If neither Osric nor Myfanwy could aid her the physicians would not avail her. Myfanwy brought a cordial to cool the fever when you were ill—I am sure it helped you.'

Alvar sighed. 'I saw many skilled doctors on my travels, Elspeth, but none of them had any knowledge of the mind. I sent potions and powders from far off lands to Myfanwy, but nothing was of any use. And then the disease began to blister on Megan's skin—and I knew the Baron had poisoned her body as well as her mind. Myfanwy kept it from me for as long as she could, but when I brought you home to Alvar, it was no longer possible to hide it. The night you saw me leaving the tower with Myfanwy she persuaded me to look at Megan again, pretending that she was suddenly much recovered. When we got there Megan was sleeping. I knew Myfanwy had lied to me, but I did not know why until you ran away . . .'

Elspeth felt the sting of tears behind her eyes. 'And I would not listen to you—forgive me, my dearest lord.'

At last she understood the terrible secret which had haunted Alvar for so many years, the agony of mind he must have endured at having to keep Megan a prisoner of the lonely tower. How often he must have been tempted to end the poor creature's misery by the sword—and yet he had not done it, even when his own happiness was threatened.

Elspeth could no longer blame him for seeking what comfort he could in Myfanwy's arms. She understood now why he could not send Megan's sister away despite the tension it had caused between them—and yet Myfanwy had believed she was to be sent away!

The question lingered in Elspeth's mind, but she would not ask it. If Alvar had been driven to the edge of murder for her sake, let it be forgotten in the mists of time. Fate had stepped in and saved him this final torment of his soul. His hands were not stained with Megan's blood. The past was gone, washed away by the swirling tides.

She looked up at her husband, smiling. Feeling the child kick in her womb, she drew his hand downward to her swollen belly. 'It is over, my love,' she whispered. 'The future lies here with our child.'

Alvar looked down at her, love chasing the shadows from his blue eyes. Eyes that were as warm and clear as a summer sky. 'Then we had best make haste and summon a priest to wed us, Elspeth—for I think my son is in a hurry to be born!'